# TRAVELING TO INFINITY
## And Other Stories

EAMON BRIGHT

### Sunset Moon

My name is Sarai Dallen, and I was the last person to be transferred to the lunar colony. All the others are dead. Of course, the record-keepers aren't proud of this unfortunate thread in the tapestry, but I've written it down anyway, in the hope that someone will find it. A small hope, I know, but it's possible.

I don't need to remind readers of problems that, by the time this record is found, will be almost as distant as the first moon landing was to me. But it's enough to say that the upheavals of the 22nd century warranted the recommission of the lunar colony. What had been marked by the record-keepers at the first landing morphed into the expected resort, and then into a substandard section of space. When the planners in the stratosphere decided to bring back the colony's marker status, they used the old automated resort shuttles to send us there.

"You'll be doing great work for the planet, Dr. Dallen," they told me. "Even in these trying times, we're sending only the best to revitalize the colony."

I knew they were lying. The others, the trusting ones, they could convince—but not me. Why send a single-occupant shuttle to the moon for a recolonizing mission? As they strapped me into the shuttle and double-checked my preset destination coordinates, I debated asking them when the latest transmission from the colony had been received.

"We don't have time for questions, doctor," they insisted, the words crackling through my intercom. "Once you reach orbit, contact ground control with your query."

I remember looking through the shuttle shielding at the blood-orange curve of the moon. Why they decided to initiate the transfer at night, I never found out. But I switched off the static from communications, and I decided not to ask for the latest transmission. Whatever I found at the colony would be there, whether I inquired about it or not.

I don't remember much about the transfer itself. Shuttle transfers, even single-occupancy automated ones, were too routine. Aside from that, I'd done enough work with my father's antique to know my way around a shuttle. I toyed with a plan to recalibrate the automated program to a different destination, but the shuttle had been rigged to self-destruct pending course changes. Once I reached the colony, I also discovered that the shuttle had been rigged to self-destruct within twenty minutes upon landing.

"Another concession to the planners in the stratosphere," I thought, as I scrambled out of the shuttle and ran for the base. I knew the temporary atmosphere would only be maintained until I reached the dome, and I didn't want to risk extinction at this early stage—not until I'd explored the base.

Under the safety of the dome, I watched the shuttle return to the elements. The temporary atmosphere around the shuttle collapsed, and I watched fragments join the rest of the space dust scattered across the surface.

"Time to join the other colonists," I muttered. "Looks like we're going to be stranded here for a while."

I could have activated the scanners to locate the other colonists, but I wanted to find them without machines, if possible. I'd spent my life around computers—even my enemies recognize my expertise—but I wanted some old-fashioned exploration for once. Maybe that was my mistake. Before I exited the pressurization chamber, I did check atmospheric and gravitational conditions for the rest of the dome. They registered normal, so I stepped out into one of the observation stations.

"Hello?" I called. "It's Dr. Sarai Dallen, the newest colonist. Anyone here?"

No one answered, even when I repeated the message on the intercom. It didn't take me long to search the rest of the stations. They were just as empty.

"Hello?" My voice was beginning to sound like an echo. "Hello, control?"

As I stepped into the control room in the center of the dome, the temperature dropped. Not too cold for a regulation suit, but cool enough to notice. At least the computer was running in control, drowning out the eerie silences in observation.

"Voice recognition Sarai Dallen, code six epsilon William four." I took a deep breath. The code was familiar, a stabilizing factor in what was obviously becoming an atypical transfer.

"Recognition successful," the computer announced. "Specify information required."

"Location of other colonists on base," I said, even though I already knew the answer.

"No other colonists on base." After a pause in the relay, the computer added, "Dome is automatically maintained from the surface of the planet."

"I don't need a machine to tell me that," I said. "What other maintenance is possible, if I'm the only one here?" Before the computer could formulate a reply, I resumed command tone. "Release all colony logs to control center."

The computer didn't respond, so I repeated the command. Finally, the relay dropped through. "All colony logs require decoding. Please offer encryption code."

"I wasn't the one who encrypted these logs! How am I supposed to know what the—"

"Encryption codes of the programmer are required to confirm decode. Without encryption codes, the logs will be erased."

The computer whirred, and I took another deep breath. I almost flipped the switch to send a query to ground control, but, fortunately, I decided to run some of my own thoughts first.

"They know I'm a computer specialist. They know I could crack codes with half my brain, if I wanted. So they want to encode the logs? Fine. Call up coded chains!"

I directed the last words to the computer, which took three relays to display the coded chains. I studied the data for no more than a minute, my brain automatically clicking the patterns into place. Another minute, and I fed the proper encryption codes into the computer.

"Almost too easy," I whispered, as the logs blinked into shape on the monitor. "The planners wanted me decode that."

But I scrolled through the logs anyway, until I found one stamped with identification for a prominent scientist.

"So that's where Crayfe disappeared to," I said, watching his visual pixelate. "I wonder if he—"

"I'm here alone," his record cut in. "Don't know if there should be other colonists here. Sent to work on artificial atmospheres, they told me. Systems are holding by automation, but—"

Dr. Crayfe's record disintegrated to gray pixels. I searched for another record, a minor planner who had been a childhood friend of my mother's.

"Georgia Marr here," she said, the flickering record still picking up the catch in her breath. "I'm not sure why my colleagues sent me here. I'm not a scientist or a technician, but the dome seems unstable. Every time—"

Her record faded like Dr. Crayfe's. I scrolled back to the most recent log and selected the entry, one by a record-keeper.

"Thomas O'Sheen, to the next colonist. If you know anything about me or my fellows, you know we like records a bit more—concrete. Good luck, whoever you are."

His record didn't fade, but it didn't continue, either. "End of record," the computer beeped. "Dome temperature dropping to specified range."

"Dome temperature dropping?" I echoed. "Where's that in the program?"

The computer didn't answer, and I shivered. Last day I was this cold, I leaned they had singled me out for the shuttle.

"Forget about sitting and waiting," I reminded myself. "Do something here, now." I redirected my focus to the monitor. "Engage thermal reaction."

"Thermal reactors are locked," the computer informed me. "Further commands of this nature will decrease dome temperature."

Ignoring another shiver, I activated the reserve thermal circuit in my suit. Once I could bend my fingers, I accessed the computer's data stream without a verbal command.

"Temperature dropping into second specified range," the computer droned.

"But I didn't ask—never mind. Send data stream to observation station four."

"All observation stations have been sealed. Data stream is locked."

I dropped into the chair adjoining the control panel, my elbows bent against my knees. "The planners must have locked it. But without the data stream, I can't stabilize the dome."

I didn't intend to vocalize my thoughts, but the computer picked up my audio. "Correct. Dome will destabilize in—"

"No, wait!" I tried not to shout, but the words echoed. "What command triggered the temperature drop?"

"Log decoding triggered temperature drop. Destabilizing in—"

"So delete the logs," I snapped. "Reverse psychology on a computer, or nothing will work."

The computer didn't appear to process the psychological remark. After an unusually long relay, it confirmed deletion of the logs, adding, "Temperature rising to former range."

I switched off my suit's thermal regulator. If any attempt to recover information meant destabilization of the dome, I was going to need that regulator at some point. Of course, not even a thermal regulator would keep me alive for long, pending the level of destabilization.

"The planners must have rigged the dome," I whispered, indifferent to the computer now. "But if I can't get records—"

In retrospect, I'm more than surprised that I didn't make the connection sooner, but it finally clicked. Thomas O'Sheen, record-keeper, hadn't stored his logs in the computer.

I assumed command tone. "Location of any concrete on the base?"

"No concrete on base," returned the computer.

I stifled a sigh. "Concrete is antiquated. Maybe—alternate 'base' connotation from 'center of operations' to 'foundation.' Give base composition."

After reeling off the expected metallic compounds, I registered 'lunar rock' from the computer's list.

"Analyze lunar rock under control center," I said, holding a mental breath. "Restrict to location of hollow spaces."

"One, under sigma plating panel. Temperature rising to specified range."

I almost laughed. "So you're trying to keep me from finding the written records now? Just what are you hiding?"

The computer didn't answer, and I knew the coolant in my suit was limited.

"Freeze lunar rock analysis," I called, "and eliminate command sequence."

I felt the temperature stabilize. At the moment, I almost abandoned hope of survival. If the computer threatened me at every command, how practical was resistance? Still, I wanted one last attempt.

For now, I'm leaving these pages here, in the spy-worthy notebook from the sole of my space boot. If my reprogramming gamble breaks the bank, I'll come back to write it down. Instructions may be obsolete,  pending I'm still alive by the time the next colonist lands. If not, at least you'll know that the planners sent you here, nonconformist single file, to be eliminated.

There's probably a poet among the planners who decided to send us here when the moon shows a sunset.

## *Blood Moon*

Unfortunately, I was standing near the window of the lunar dome when the single-occupancy shuttle landed—and I only say that in retrospect. Had I realized Marcus was aboard that shuttle, I might have failed to extend the temporary atmosphere that allowed him to reach the dome. We all look roughly the same in our regulation suits, and I was, to be completely honest, more interested in the state of the shuttle than the arrival of another colonist.

His shuttle, unlike mine, hadn't disintegrated after landing. While he slipped into the airlock, I listened to the hiss of the depressurizing mechanisms and studied the shuttle. Just before the airlock opened, I punched a series of buttons in the nearest control panel, and a lift-equipped lunar bot rumbled out to stow the shuttle inside the hangar adjoining the dome.

"Good boy, Rover," I said, allowing myself a smile.

"Haven't stopped naming your bots, I see." Marcus spoke from behind me, slightly breathless. "And Rover? Not too original."

"True," I replied, keeping my words clipped and precise, "but I've been on solitary assignment here for almost a year, and there are only so many pieces of equipment in the dome."

Marcus held out his still-gloved hands. "If you can believe it, it's a pleasure to see you."

I shook my head. "Our relationship would alter for the better if we ceased to communicate."

Before he could reply, I drifted down the hall into the center of the dome, towards computer control. I'd dropped the artificial gravity just below normal, and I imagined Marcus gliding awkwardly along behind me.

"I did hope," he said, "that we might at least include common courtesy in our relationship. If I understood the cryptic instructions from ground control, we're going to be the sole occupants of this dome for quite some time."

"No, I've been the sole occupant of this dome for quite some time," I corrected, settling into my usual chair and running a cursory diagnostic on the computer. "From what I understand, I wasn't expected to survive my first day here."

He seated himself carefully. "That's what the planners told me. They said you had all failed your assignments, and the colony was empty." I just heard his next words over the hum of the computer. "I hoped their information was incorrect."

I sighed. "They weren't all lies. When I arrived here, the colony was in fact empty."

"Empty?" he repeated. " Richard Crayfe, and Georgia Marr, and Tom O'Sheen—gone?"

I tried to ignore the sound of his voice breaking. "Don't ask for sympathy. I was able to retrieve some of their records, but they're definitely deceased."

He took a deep breath. "How? If they failed their assignments, they should have returned to Earth."

I turned my chair to face his. "Do you really think, after all this time, the planners would allow that? You, of all people, should know the risk involved in defying them."

"So you blame me for your lonely year?" He shook his head. "I didn't ask you to join me."

"Does it matter that I didn't join you?" I scanned the results of the diagnostic, highlighting code to edit. "My simple association with you earned me a showdown with this killer computer."

He chuckled. "That was their mistake, wasn't it? It's clearly not a killer computer now."

I didn't laugh along with him. "Obviously, no. O'Sheen left some genuine paper records under the sigma plating panel. Just his version of Theseus and the Labyrinth, but that gave me an idea. I reprogrammed the beast into an impossible maze of code."

He held up his hands. "Don't try to explain the technical gibberish to me."

"I wasn't about to," I said, "but, just for that, you get the short version." Pointing to the highlighted lines of code in the diagnostic, I added, "For a computer, this code is the equivalent of a logical contradiction. It's so busy trying to solve the contradiction that the programming loops into itself, keeping the dome running. As long as I don't antagonize it by trying to retrieve classified information, it lets me get on my with my life."

"Classified information?" he repeated. "Such as?"

"Such as the colonists' logs," I said. "My first day here, I retrieved partial extracts while the computer alternately tried to freeze and melt me."

"Why risk your life for the logs?" he asked, staring at the lines of computer code.

"To find out what happened to them," I said, editing the code with brief touches to the screen. "They were your colleagues. Wouldn't you take the same risk?"

Out of habit, I held my breath as the computer accepted my changes to the Labyrinth. I knew Marcus was watching me, but I didn't look up.

"Can I see Tom's records?" he asked. "It's been a long time."

I considered refusing, but his request was almost a plea. Despite my better judgement, I assumed command tone. "Labyrinth, release the key."

A narrow panel in the console retracted, revealing a neat sheaf of creased paper. I slipped on gloves before handing it to Marcus, who still wore his regulation suit. Leaving the panel open, I turned to run a final diagnostic on the edited computer code.

I'd almost forgotten he was sitting there until he spoke. "Tom had the neatest handwriting," he said, "except for what he called his 'story hand.' All full of flourishes, like something out of an old manuscript." He laughed. "Georgia always tried to copy him, but she never could."

"And this is his 'story hand'?" I asked, squinting at the pages. "I was glad he gave Ariadne a real part, but the handwriting's not bad."

"I'm glad it could be of use to somebody," he said, handing the papers to me. "I never could read it that easily."

I slid the papers back behind the panel. "Finally something you had to work for?"

He slipped off his gloves and laced his fingers together. "Tom's handwriting was the least of my challenges, Dr. Dallen. Don't try to pretend you don't know that." I started to respond, but he shook his head. "I think we've had enough. There's another challenge facing both of us, and cooperation is the key to success."

I checked that the diagnostic showed clear. "The only challenge I foresee is storing up enough patience strap you in your shuttle."

Marcus tried to laugh. "Don't you want to leave? It won't take much to convert the shuttle to double-occupancy. I'm sure—"

"I'm sure the planners will send us back, with a double shuttle that explodes on-route," I said. "If I had to guess, they only left yours intact because they knew you'd be a particularly easy target for the unmodified Labyrinth."

"Our challenge still stands," he insisted. "If the planners don't know you've tamed the computer, we can establish a base of operations in the dome. Every colonist they send will already be predisposed to join our cause."

"Our cause?" I laughed. "You want to revive the cause that killed Crayfe, and Georgia, and Tom? The cause that almost killed me? Not while I run this dome."

"It's the perfect scenario," he insisted. "The planners will be supplying their own downfall."

"Too perfect," I objected. "They would uncover your plots eventually. They always do, remember? Why else would you be here now?"

He leaned forward in his chair. His voice deepened slightly, and I realized I couldn't look away. "For the cause, Dr. Dallen," he said. "For the cause, every sacrifice is meaningful."

I struck out with my fists, almost before I realized it. I didn't hit Marcus, but his chair slipped backwards.

"Was Crayfe's death meaningful?" I asked, forcing out the words. "Or Georgia's? Or Tom's? What about my mother's sacrifice?"

"Your mother," Marcus said slowly, "has nothing to do with the cause. You're famous for seeing things impartially, aren't you? If you examine the facts—"

I nodded. "Of course. My mother meant nothing to you. We won't discuss her."

He drew in his breath like a cadet who'd been winded during combat training. "Again," he finally said, "your mother has nothing to do with it. But you won't join the cause, will you?" He maneuvered his chair closer to the control panel, tapping the edge with his fingers.

"I won't stay here and watch my dome overflow with fanatics, if that's what you envision," I said, pushing back from the control panel and out of my chair. "I'd rather face an Earth full of planners, so that's where I'll go."

I heard him stop tapping. "No," he said. "I don't think you will."

At first, I thought the thermal regulators in the dome had malfunctioned, but the temperature display read stable—and I was still shivering.

Behind me, Marcus assumed command tone. "Labyrinth, voice recognition Marcus Dallen, code six William epsilon five. Following ten-minute countdown, reactivate Minotaur."

I turned. "Dad, please!" My voice broke, and I couldn't steady it. "Please don't."

My father might have smiled at me. "I'm sorry, Sarai. The planners scanned the dome remotely and realized that you survived. If I hadn't agreed to eliminate you—"

"They'd eliminate you too," I whispered.

His shoulders lifted slightly. "My supply of charm finally ran out. They weren't willing to give me any other terms."

"Nine minutes until Minotaur reactivation," the computer announced. "Dome destabilization pending."

I knew I should begin rewriting the Minotaur code. My previous battles with the computer meant that I could theoretically solve another crisis, but I didn't move. After a moment or two, I felt his hand on my shoulder. For whatever reason, I didn't shrug it away.

"Sarai," he said softly. "Believe it or not, I think we're working for the same objective—and I'm not thinking of my cause, or even your code."

"What do you know about my objectives?" I asked. "Mine made sense, and yours never did."

"That's exactly my point," he said, turning to face me. "Your lines of logical code and my endless appeals for the cause are very different things. Could you think beyond them, just for a moment?"

"Eight minutes," the computer informed us. "Evacuation of non-targets is advised."

I almost laughed. "I don't have many moments left. Do you think the computer will freeze my cells, or incinerate them? Maybe both, if I'm unlucky."

"Sarai, please." Both his hands were on my shoulders now, trembling like his voice.

"Now who's pleading?" I was too close not to see the tears on his cheeks, but I couldn't help the retort. "Why didn't you ask me before activating the Minotaur, Dad?"

He didn't answer, but the computer noted the seven-minute mark.

"Okay, I'll answer," I said, shaking my shoulders free. "We're both incredibly stubborn people, so you thought a life-or-death situation would force us to have this conversation."

His smile almost seemed subdued. "It was the perfect scenario." He scrubbed away his tears, and I noticed just how worn his face was.

"You're starting to look like Grandad," I blurted. "You really are."

He laughed. "There's the honesty I was looking for."

"Six minutes," the computed droned. "Six minutes."

"Here's a question," he said. "Do you really enjoy all our back-and-forth?"

"Are you implying that I have an emotional core hidden somewhere?" I asked, and he laughed harder. "But, as long as we're being honest, no."

"Well," he said, "in that case, would you consider—"

I held up my hand. "This doesn't mean I'm ready to hand you a clean slate. I expect answers about my mother, and about this stunt the planners convinced you to pull—not to mention an explanation on behalf of Crayfe, and Georgia, and Tom O'Sheen."

"Five minutes to destabilization," the computer insisted.

I glanced at the console. "Pending that I can recode the Minotaur in five minutes."

For the first time, he looked worried. "I was counting on that," he admitted. "And on convincing the remote scanners that I've eliminated you."

I bent over the console, mentally sorting the flashing code chains. "My last record was four fifty-five. If I can beat that, reconfiguring any remote scanning indicators will be easy." After only half a minute, I fed the new code chains into the Labyrinth.

"Recoding denied," the computer announced. "Destabilization pending."

I tried not to slam my fist into the console. "It was clearly too simple," I admitted. "They must have scanned all my stored code. None of the reconfigured chains will work."

Then I heard him laugh, the laugh that meant a crazy idea was about to come spilling out.

"Is this a viable idea?" I asked. "Not all of yours were."

He shook his head. "It's not mine—it's from Tom's story. Ariadne followed Theseus into the Labyrinth, and she distracted the Minotaur. The beast couldn't decide which target to attack, so Theseus dispatched it from behind."

I blinked. "How exactly does that help us? We have just under four minutes."

"You have to give the Minotaur another contradiction," he said. "If you force it to activate, force it to simultaneously raise and lower the temperature in the dome, it won't know which command to execute."

"While I hate to admit it," I said, queuing up a string of new code, "you may be right. If it's confused enough, I could reroute it into—"

"Three minutes," the computer interrupted. "Destabilization pending."

I took a deep breath and looked at my father. "Should I do it? There's no guarantee."

He nodded. "Sarai, even if it fails, I'll consider this mission a success."

I allowed myself a smile and assumed command tone. "Labyrinth, voice recognition Sarai Dallen, code six William epsilon four. Combine Minotaur destruct codes seven beta and eleven delta. Override countdown and activate."

Lights flashed, and the computer whirred. "Ten-second countdown mandated. Destruct codes combined. Dome destabilization beginning in ten, nine—"

"And just to be sure," I whispered, "we're rerouting the Minotaur into the hangar."

He had been counting along with the computer, but he stopped and stared at me. "We're what?"

Before I could answer, the computer spoke. "Program rerouted. Hangar overloading."

The walls of the dome didn't admit sound waves, but we watched as the hangar's monitor displayed an internal explosion. Fragments of the shuttle skittered across the floor, and Rover rolled in all directions, extinguishing fires.

"Minotaur activated," the computed announced, but I hardly heard.

"Why in all of blazing space did the shuttle explode?" I asked, giving him a long stare.

He buried his face in his hands. "I think I must have left some circuits running."

I took a shaky breath. "And any sudden temperature change would overload that decommissioned machinery, especially if the Minotaur tried to heat the hangar first."

"I'm glad neither of us decided to retreat to the hangar," he said, "but our problems aren't over."

"Really?" I noted—impartially—that this remark wasn't a retort. "And the Minotaur wasn't enough?"

"We're going to have to communicate with some courtesy if you want to repurpose the shuttle," he said. "It's a task designed for two, so I'm afraid you won't get the relationship alteration that you wanted."

"I'll get stories to rival Tom O'Sheen's instead," I reminded him. "You still owe me several explanations."

He nodded. "Now that the Minotaur has run to ground, we should have plenty of time."

"Not if the planners realize the stunt we pulled," I pointed out. Leaning over the console, I initiated three stealth-scan programs simultaneously. "Then they'll send out the reprogrammers in style."

He chuckled. "You could outsmart the whole fleet without trying."

My laugh, the kind that meant I was in fact amused, escaped before I could catch it. "Between Dr. Sarai Dallen and her impossible father, they wouldn't stand a chance."

## Mission 404

Department of Extraplanetary Exploration
Classified Transcript
Solar Date: 25 May 2160

D7, base of operations has lost visual. Repeat, base has lost visual. D7, acknowledge.

*Delta seven, acknowledging. Is the audio clear? Acknowledge, please.*

Your audio is clear, D7. Describe your surroundings for the record.

*Surroundings haven't changed since visual shorted out. Repeat, surroundings haven't changed.*

Relay current readings in lieu of description. Describe changes in density of asteroid field.

*No change. Asteroids still orbiting at constant rate. Relaying current readings now.*

Readings received. Information will be correlated momentarily. Proceed to base, D7.

*Acknowledged. Entering flight plan back to—wait, new data registering in sensor relays.*

Forward new information to base databanks. Specify new information.

*Looks like a solar flare's heating up. If I can't maneuver away, the shuttle will feel it.*

Data has been received. Recommendation, to proceed to base. Repeat, proceed to base.

*Acknowledged—but I'm in the middle of an asteroid field, so proceeding will take time.*

Recommendation, to proceed to base. Repeat, proceed to base.

*I've been relaying with a computer, haven't I? Can't I get a human being on the line?*

Negative. All on-duty personnel have been reassigned to crisis stations.

*Are you telling me they left shuttle communications to a computer?*

Affirmative. D7 is currently the sole exploratory craft launched from cruiser *Titan*.

*So it wasn't worth it to give one shuttle a personal relay?*

Affirmative. Cruiser systems are designed to function at peak efficiency.

*Isn't there anyone remotely humanoid listening to this? Acknowledge.*

[ ... ]

*Bridge? Engineering? Infirmary? I'll even take Recreation, if there's someone there.*

[ ... ]

*That solar flare is starting to catch the shuttle. Either an asteroid gets me, or—*

Hello? D7, can you acknowledge?

*Delta seven, acknowledging. Have I reached a human? Who is this?*

Infirmary, responding to your call. What's your condition?

*Infirmary? Since when did Infirmary monitor communications?*

I had a free minute and picked up your signal. My crisis station is always here.

*Cruiser's condition must be compromised, if crisis stations were activated.*

Engineering would be more exact, but I'm sure it's less than optimal.

*And that means you won't be helping me.*

[ ... ]

*Anyone been to Infirmary yet? From what I hear, you haven't seen many this trip.*

Negative. If enough systems fail, we'll be seeing them.

*System failure? Well, as long as it's not Engineering,* Titan *will pull through.*

From what I've been picking up on the intercom, the solar flare has been affecting—

*No, don't tell me. My own engines will be overloading in a minute.*

Can you maneuver out of the asteroid field before that happens?

*The flare's compromised my sensors, and flying this thing without data is a risk.*

Well, it's either blow up or burn up, isn't it?

*You're not very cheerful—but you're right. I'm surprised my audio is still relaying.*

[ … ]

*Hello? Anyone there? Infirmary, acknowledge.*

Yes, sorry. Infirmary acknowledging. I think Engineering was experimenting with options.

*You mean cut communications to supply the engines? What good would that do?*

They might try skipping directly to lightspeed, to bypass the flare.

*And leave me here? With an untapped asteroid field to log, all by myself? Inconsiderate.*

Didn't catch that last part. Could you repeat?

*It's not important. But if you are shifting to lightspeed, don't tell me.*

Easier to die a hero's death that way? That's a risk you scientists take.

*I wish the risk was bigger than an asteroid field. Why bother dying for rocks?*

Would you prefer *Titan* to be full of cadets? Or interplanetary committees?

*Definitely not interplanetary committees. They never act, just talk.*

Cadets? A cruiser full of undertrained, overworked youngsters bleeding adrenaline?

*See, that would be a reason to strand me. What's one scientist over a bunch of kids?*

Oh, I just treat the patients. Asking the hard questions isn't my department.

*Any chance you can get this patient back onboard? I'll even try maneuvering blind.*

Engineering's still debating the lightspeed skip. They don't want to disrupt the field.

*Captain thinks a handful of asteroids is more important than cruiser personnel?*

Or someone up the chain does. Why bring a cruiser to analyze the field?

*They need a data correlation system, and most exploratory craft aren't equipped.*

But while you're forwarding data to *Titan*, this flare shows up.

*I don't think the field and the flare are connected. Could have deployed more shuttles, though.*

Why? One asteroid field too much for you?

*No, but it's some of the strangest data I've ever—hang on, maneuver in progress.*

Better proceed to base of operations before *Titan* skips off. I think we might be on the move.

*Been eavesdropping on Engineering? If they don't get it right—*

Then *Titan* will take a lightspeed skip right into the flare. Did the computer collect all data?

*I think I relayed everything. It didn't ask for anything else, told me to proceed to base.*

[ . . . ]

*Infirmary? Are you still there? Acknowledge, please.*

Infirmary, acknowledging. They're cutting communications in a minute, to reroute power.

[ . . .]

D7, acknowledge. Is your shuttle compromised?

*Negative. In fact, I just cleared an asteroid. Not that it matters, since the data's relayed.*

If you maneuver quickly, we may be able to pull you in before—

*I know how far I am from* Titan. *There's not enough time. They don't need me.*

I can plead a medical emergency, delay them for a few minutes—

*And risk compromising* Titan*? I don't think so. These asteroids are—*

Have you been compromised? D7, can you hear me?

*Affirmative. I was racing the flare, but an asteroid just took me out of the running.*

Can you maneuver? I'll pull someone from crisis station to calculate the distance—

*Doesn't matter. Engines are overloading. You'll be in lightspeed soon.*

You're still a member of the crew, and Infirmary is responsible for your safety.

*You want to do something for me? Tell me your name.*

[ ... ]

*Infirmary, acknowledge. Please, I know you have a name.*

It's David. My name's David.

*Listen, David. I want you to find out why these asteroids are so important.*

I'm only from Infirmary. How would I know what to do?

*Make my risk worth something. Find out. The data was encoded before it was correlated.*

I'm not a computer scientist, D7. Just a doctor.

*Then find someone who is. Gather a group, if you have to.*

Sounds like extraplanetary espionage to me. I want to help you, but—

*David, do you want my death to mean something? I told you, that data is—*

D7, acknowledge. We've lost your audio. Repeat, D7, acknowledge.

[ ... ]

Acknowledge, D7. Please, acknowledge.

[ ... ]

Computer, status report for shuttle D7.

*Shuttle D7 has been destroyed. Repeat, shuttle D7 has been destroyed.*

## *Resolution*

"Dr. Lancaster, thank you for coming." Director Langton smiled as he spoke, but David nodded in response.

"It's a pleasure to visit the Department for Extraplanetary Exploration," he said, seating himself on the edge of his chair and bracing his feet against the carpeted floor.

Langton smiled again. "You're one of many who hold that opinion, I'm sure." Leaning back in his chair, he added, "We don't get many people from Medical up here, you know. Perhaps you made an appointment just for the pleasure of seeing me?"

David refused to laugh. "Of course, Director Langton. Of course."

Langton chuckled. "Flattery will only get you so far—but now that travel beyond Earth's confines is possible, you could go very far indeed."

"I have been, sir." David looked behind Langton to the photographs hanging on his wall. "In fact, I've just returned from a mission with the cruiser *Titan*, in that exact system."

Langton glanced over his shoulder. "Beautiful, isn't it? I'm sure the cartographers enjoyed drawing up their maps."

"As much as they ever enjoyed mapping a single-star system without satellites," David said.

Langton smile dimmed, and he reached inside his desk drawer for a tablet. "Agreeing with everything I say would defeat the purpose of a discussion, doctor."

David reached for his pen, remembered that he had left his lab coat behind, and dropped his hand. "Was I repeating, sir? I wasn't aware that we should be having a discussion."

Langton began scanning the tablet. "David Lancaster. Medical officer, first class. Specialization in neuroscience. Commendations for exemplary service—"

"Please, sir." David leaned forward in his chair. "Extend flattery to me, by all means."

Langton slid the tablet into his desk drawer and smiled. "I'm sure there's a commendation included for diplomatic speech, but I won't embarrass you."

David realized he was mimicking Langton's smile. "My profound thanks, sir."

For a moment, Langton didn't speak. "My assistant informed me," he resumed, "that you've just returned from your fourth extraplanetary mission. Perhaps you're seeking an alternate occupation after so many years in service, perhaps even here in the department?"

David glanced at Langton's pictures again. "Perhaps. This last mission made clear that space travel can bring any personnel into situations of great risk."

Langton laughed. "Surely that fact formed the basis of your most elementary training?" Then he sighed. "I understand, doctor. The department constantly balances possible risk with possible success, and decisions can be—wearying."

"I'm sure that's true," David said, "but all your decisions must be correctly balanced."

Langton nodded. "We pride ourselves on consistently correct conclusions." He chuckled. "I should report that to Marketing."

"Certainly," David said. "But I'm not in Marketing. I'm in Medical, and Medical decided that one of the department's conclusions should be confirmed."

"Confirmed?" Langton repeated. "In what way? Medical should have no reason to doubt."

David smiled. "Surely your assistant showed you Medical's clearance papers? We have evidence that the permanent decommission of a *Titan* crewmember is connected—in a minor capacity, of course—to a command decision effected through this department."

Langton stared at his photographs before turning back to David. "We'll be more than happy to accommodate Medical's request, if you'll produce the evidence."

David reached into his suit pocket. "Pardon the paper, sir, but the evidence was only available in old-fashioned form."

Langton reached across his desk and unfolded the paper square. As Langton read, David planted his feet more firmly against the carpet. He noticed the steady hum of the intercom, and the pulse of his own heartbeat. When Langton reached up to activate the intercom, he caught his breath.

"Nothing to be worried about, doctor," Langton said, with another smile. "I'm only requesting the complete files for Mission 404." Moments later, his assistant brought in a tablet, which he scanned.

"I admire your efficiency," David said, satisfied that his breathing had returned to standard rhythm. "Your assistant must keep extensive files, ready to be read at a moment's notice."

Langton looked up from the tablet. "The department insists that we retain complete files. You're certain that your evidence pertains to Mission 404?"

David nodded. "The data from the asteroid belt should match the data in your files—unless I've been mistaken."

Langton shook his head. "You've been commendably thorough—but you have missed a slight detail. Only a slight detail, of course."

David reminded himself to breathe. "And what slight detail would that be?"

Langton pointed to the tablet, prompting David to lean over the desk. "You'll notice that the pilot of shuttle D7—the permanently decommissioned pilot—was Peter Dallen."

David glanced up at Langton. "And the pilot's name is a relevant detail, I'll assume?"

Langton shook his head and smiled. "Dr. Lancaster, don't you remember your history? The Dallen family was known for—"

"I fail to see how Peter Dallen's ancestry is relevant," David interrupted. "He was—permanently decommissioned—in connection with the Department of Extraplanetary Exploration. You won't deny facts, will you? Think of the department's reputation."

Langton's smile hardened. "The department is not in the business of denying facts, doctor."

David tried to laugh. "And I would never imply that you were. Since the department does deal in facts, I may be interested—slightly interested, of course—in knowing what those facts are."

Langton chuckled. "Dr. Lancaster, I fail to see what interest Medical would have in the facts of Peter Dallen's permanent decommission. As you doubtless already know, he was collecting data from an asteroid belt when a solar flare incapacitated his shuttle. The department merely balanced the risks—the loss of asteroid data over Peter Dallen."

David nodded. "And any member of the service should be able to discern the department's motives for doing so?"

Langton nodded. "Of course, doctor, of course."

David stood up, rocking his chair backwards. "Then I'm afraid I've encroached on too much of your valuable time, sir. Please accept my apologies."

He reached for the square of paper, but Langton slid his tablet over it. "I believe we'll retain this data," he said. "It will be a valuable addition to the information concerning Mission 404."

David waited a moment too long before answering. "Always happy to be of service to the department, sir. It's been a pleasure."

Langton smiled. "A pleasure, Dr. Lancaster. A true pleasure."

## Connection

*December 12, 2151—8:57 A.M.*

"So I decided to walk right into the Department and ask for Director Langton, like some clueless cadet, and they actually let me see him. I meant to ferret out answers like the board on examination day, but we were practically skating around each other. Neither of us admitting anything, and—James, are you even listening to me?"

I glanced up from reviewing the day's dossiers. "Sure, David, sure. But we've got more patients to maintain than you've got stories to tell. Maybe later?"

David laughed. "Okay, you weren't listening. The minute we're off the clock, you're getting the whole story." He paused, glanced at the dossiers, and grinned. "You'll take the top one, I assume?"

Just like that, my tongue refused to function. "Well, I thought—I thought—"

David kept grinning. "As you said, we've got patients to maintain." He grabbed the rest of the dossiers, leaving me with the one labeled *McRoy*. "Have fun with your section of the antique shop, James."

He was out the door and down the corridor before I could protest that our floor wasn't actually an antique shop. Sure, our patients were much older than most, technically speaking, but I doubted that they would appreciate being referred to as antiques. If he hadn't left me with the McRoy dossier, I would have chased him down and debated the point—but he had. I stared at the tablet in my hands until the heading pixelated.

"Come on, come on," I muttered. "How hard can it be? You've done this every day for over a year now."

Tucking the tablet under my arm, I paced down the corridor until I reached the room marked with the name on my dossier. The identification system collected my fingerprint and retinal scan before the door swung open.

"Anderson, James," the computer intoned. "Medical, first class. Reporting for duty."

"As always," I said. As usual, no one responded. I glanced around the room, ensuring that all monitors were sounding a steady rhythm. "That must mean we're all dandy, doesn't it?"

The doctor I was relieving stared at me. "Do you always talk to them like that?" she asked, gathering her medical kit and stepping out of the monitoring station. "You know they can't hear you."

I shrugged. "Who else is there to talk to? Everyone's allowed their quirks."

She shook her head. "Well, you can have yours. I need coffee."

I stepped into the monitoring station. "Enjoy your coffee—and have a wonderful day."

She stopped on her way out the door to stare at me again. "I think the time with the antiques is affecting you. No one says that anymore, Anderson. And it's too early in the morning for smiles."

"You'll feel better after coffee," I said. "No matter the era, that stuff is constant."

She raised her eyebrows. "Whatever you say. I'm clocking out now."

The identification system beeped, the door swung open, and she left. For the next six hours, it would be just me and the antiques—the patients. I logged a cursory review of the monitoring system, then circled the room to check each pod individually. Under their glass domes, the faces of the McRoy family never changed—all part of a timeless peace that had lasted nearly a century and a half.

"I won't actually talk to you all day," I whispered, "but I could ask so many questions."

I paused at Rob McRoy's pod. I'd always wanted to know why he chose to put his family in suspended animation. Concern over the upheavals of the 21st century? Hope for a potentially brighter future? Desire for uncertain adventures? His choice was either incredibly brave, or incredibly foolish, or both.

I stopped to adjust the controls for Annette McRoy's pod. I'd always liked to think that she and her husband came to a joint decision on suspended animation. I knew she had researched the science. She must have understood that her family's chances were minimal, even under the assumption that science would advance far enough to sustain their lives indefinitely.

Jacob, Christopher, and Paul—each of the McRoy brothers kept a steady monitor. Jacob was only a few years older than I was when he entered suspension. Paul, only a few years younger, and Christopher, almost the same age. Did Christopher realize that science would have accelerated far beyond his knowledge, if he emerged to enter medical school? At least humans still enjoy music and stories. Jacob and Paul would find a place.

Loretta McRoy—I read the plaque over her pod silently. Unlike her parents and her brothers, she had been suspended with the smallest of smiles on her face, providing every doctor on the unit with a mystery. She was dressed differently, too, like a fashion plate taken several decades before her suspension. Maybe the historian took her job too seriously? That's what most of us thought. But I thought—well, I thought she looked just dandy. Did they say 'dandy' in the mid-twentieth century? I honestly wasn't sure.

*December 13, 8:58 A.M.*

"James, you won't believe this! Remember the Langton fiasco? Turns out that data I had decoded was actually—"

I handed David all the dossiers except one. "David, you already told me that story, and we still have patients to monitor. Are you sure you're not developing an obsession?"

He shook his head. "This information is relevant to our unit, I know that." Then he read through the tablets in his hands. "Did you voluntarily take the McRoy dossier?"

I fought a rush of craniofacial erythema, but I could tell by my reflection in a nearby window that my face was turning red anyway. "Haven't I taken it voluntarily before?"

David chuckled. "And you're calling me obsessed? But about that data—"

"Later, all right? I'm about to go on the clock." I started to walk down the corridor toward the McRoy room, but David followed me.

"I don't understand every detail," he said, "but that data was the key to waking up our antiques."

I stopped walking, so suddenly that David ran up against me. Tablets scattered across the hallway, and I realized my tongue was barely functioning again.

"Out of suspension?" I managed. "How?"

"The data showed that the asteroids from *Titan*'s mission contained a novel metallic-magnetic compound," David said, collecting his tablets and pushing me down the hall to the McRoy room. "The team thinks it might be the key to opening the pods."

I almost jammed my thumb against the fingerprint pad, and I couldn't hold still for the retinal scan. After the system finally acknowledged me, I held the door open and looked back at David. "If you have details, I'll be here," I said.

David grinned. "Sure, James, sure."

Ignoring the drone of the computer and the confusion of my on-duty colleague, I dropped my dossier in the monitoring station and made a cursory circle of the room. "Hear that, everybody?" I asked. "You might actually be waking up."

"You know they can't—" My colleague started to object, but I interrupted.

"Hear me, I know. But that's what I would say, if they could. Ask Lancaster. He's the one who told me. There's new data, and—"

"Have you had too much coffee, Anderson?" He gave me a thorough once-over before gathering up his kit. "Or maybe I need the coffee. Clocking out."

"Have a fantastic day," I called after him, but I don't think he heard.

After double-checking the monitoring station, I paced between Rob and Annette. She would have read the journals. She would know that the pods' designers had effectively provided a lock without a key. Or maybe there had been a key, lost somewhere in the chaos, and this compound could be another—the start to Rob's adventure.

"You wouldn't understand," I said to Paul, "but we need a way to release the pods gradually. The right metal would interact correctly with the pod, and the metallic element could effect a gentle release. I'm not sure it would make a very interesting story, though."

"And if the release is gentle enough," I told Christopher, "we should be able to stabilize you with all systems intact. Your monitors are hardly ever irregular, in any case."

"And then," I announced to Jacob, "you can keep writing your music. It probably won't be that popular—Mozart's style is practically ancient now—but you'll have at least one listener."

I paused by Loretta's pod. "Make that two," I said, "because it's going to count as historical either way, and she'll study it. I'll just listen to it because I like it."

Then the intercom on the monitoring station buzzed. "James? Can you hear me?"

I almost tripped over Loretta's monitor on my way to the station. "Yes, it's James."

David laughed. "I wasn't expecting Rob McRoy to answer. Are you sitting down?"

I dropped into a chair. "Now I am. Any news?"

"Turns out the team was much further along on this project than I thought," he said. "They didn't tell everyone, in case of utter failure, but they'll be ready to reverse suspension tomorrow."

"Oh, just dandy," I said, wondering why I couldn't come up with something else. "That's fantastic, David. Are they—are they—"

"Starting with the McRoy room?" David laughed again. "Affirmative, Anderson."

After David closed the intercom circuit, I wandered around the room until I reached Loretta's pod. I knew I was imagining it, because subjects under suspension don't alter, but I thought her smile had changed.

"Loretta," I whispered, "I don't know if you're going to like the 22nd century. We're full to the brim with science and technology and space travel—all wonderful stuff—but there's not really a market for antiques."

She kept smiling, and I grinned. "You know, it doesn't matter. You'll do just fine anywhere, and you won't care if there are no other antique collectors. You'll be the one lovely Loretta."

My last words echoed in the inevitable silence, and I realized I was blushing again. She couldn't hear me, or see me, and I was still blushing.

I sighed. "Never mind. I'll come up with something better—for all of you—by tomorrow."

*December 14, 8:59 A.M.*

"James—I wouldn't go in yet, if I were you."

David took me by the shoulder and started to turn me around, but I shrugged away his hand. "Why shouldn't I? I've been monitoring the McRoy room, and we're going to get results today."

He stepped in front of the door. "Most of the team are already in there, and they don't want to be overcrowded."

I stared at him. "They initiated the procedure already? Why wasn't I informed?"

David took the McRoy dossier from my hands and handed it to a colleague who was exiting the room. "Yes, five hours ago. They knew it would take time, and they didn't want the rest of us complicating the process."

"Why didn't this project involve the whole team?" David started to answer, but I held up my hand. "Don't tell me it's because I'm a junior member."

He shrugged. "It's the department's business. Can't you be satisfied that they planned something beneficial for once?"

I forced my voice down to reasonable levels. "David, I don't care about the Department of Extraplanetary Exploration. The McRoy family is coming out of suspension, and I want to be there."

Before David could answer, the intercom in the corridor sounded, and one of our colleagues spoke. "Suspension unit to McRoy room, stat. Second subject is destabilizing. Suspension unit to McRoy room."

I turned away from David and stared into the retinal scanner. He tried to pull me back when the door opened, but I kept moving.

"It's Annette," I said. "I know her data trend. Of the family, she would be the most likely to destabilize." I pushed past colleagues to Annette's pod, but they wouldn't allow me to adjust her monitor. "Be careful," I pleaded. "She only needs the smallest adjustments, and then—"

I felt David's hand on my shoulder. "Come on, James," he said. "Let them work."

As the crowd of colleagues parted for me, I realized the rest of the pods were empty.

"What happened?" I whispered. "Rob? Jacob? Christopher? Paul?"

David shook his head. "Not in here, James. Come on."

I didn't need a monitor to tell me that my lungs weren't functioning at normal capacity. I followed David out of the room and down several corridors without registering our direction.

"Just tell me, David," I said. "We've lost patients before. It's part of Medical."

He pushed open a door without looking at me, and I stepped inside the room. Lying in regulation hospital beds and connected to steadily beeping monitors were the rest of the McRoy family.

David turned and smiled at me. "They came out just fine. Sleeping now."

I studied the monitors. "Their breathing is better than mine," I whispered to David. "Next time you try a joke like that, you'll be in trouble."

He held out his hands. "Sorry, sorry. I thought you'd be happy to see them."

I took a deep breath. "I am, don't worry. When they wake up, I'll have plenty to say."

"Of course," David said, opening the door and stepping out. "I'll leave the speeches to you."

I looked at Rob. I would tell him that his adventure had succeeded, but that he might enter his new century without Annette. I would tell Christopher about our medical advances, Jacob about our music, Paul about all our new stories—but I would have to tell them that not even our world could guarantee Annette's life.

Then I saw Loretta stir. I turned my back and scanned blindly through the nearest tablet, wishing that I could cure my persistent craniofacial erythema. For what felt like hours, I heard nothing except my irregular heartbeat and the steady rhythm of the monitors.

"Well," I finally heard her say, "as far as I can tell, we're awake."

I turned so quickly that I almost stumbled over Rob's monitor, but I didn't speak.

"Is that right, doctor?" she asked. "Have we come out of suspension?"

I tried to open my mouth, but an inexplicable paralysis had set in.

She glanced at the other beds. "Mother's running a little late. You'll try your best to wake her? I know there's some risk."

I nodded, but my mind felt like a tablet suddenly cleared of all data.

She smiled, and I suddenly realized the meaning of that half-smile she'd kept under suspension. All symptoms pointed to a diagnosis of amusement.

"Do you have a name?" she asked. I glanced down at my identification badge, but she shook her head. "No, that only says Dr. Anderson. There's another half, isn't there?"

"Call me James," I stammered, glad that David's absence saved me from becoming an absolute embarrassment.

She was still smiling. "Because that's your name?"

"I'm Anderson," I finally managed. "James Anderson."

"You're certainly not James Bond, are you?" She pointed to the chair by her bed, and I sat down. "You'll have to say much more if you're going to give me my long-awaited history lesson."

"History." I took a deep breath and tried two words. "Of course."

"Do doctors from the future still carry pen and paper?" she asked. "Or have you progressed to better tools?" She paused, and her smile disappeared. "Have you left books behind?"

"I collect books," I said. "I could lend you some, if you like."

She smiled again. "I think I'm going to like you, James."

I wanted to say something, but the words wouldn't form. Everything I ever thought of saying to any member of the McRoy family, everything I had said during suspension, completely vanished. Finally, I heard myself say, "That's—that's just dandy."

And Loretta laughed.

### *Suspension*

She readied her paintbrush as the first bars of Dvořák's "New World" symphony spilled from her record player. The gentle hum of the strings guided her fine tip across the whitewash. When the music built to a crescendo, she stepped back and studied the wall. Her night-black line slid precisely through the mural like the decisive sweep of her imaginary conductor's baton, curving around patches of darkened green and raindrop blue. Tilting her head, she half-closed her eyes and added a final flourish to mark the end-point of her path.

Without looking behind her, she lifted the needle of the record player and shifted it closer to the center of the record. The notes from the second movement skipped slightly, but she hummed along with the record.

*Going home, going home, I'll be going home*

A ribbon of sunshine crossed through her lakes, her hills, and her path, a final golden stroke over swaths of color. She glanced up at her single window, but a cloud erased the sunbeam before she had time to smile. Patiently, she lifted her paint and settled the can in one corner of the room. At the wash-stand in the other corner, she cleaned her brush, her hands, and her face. Straightening the collar on her maroon vintage dress, she half-smiled at herself in the mirror.

*Even though the road is long, I'll be going home*

Then she stepped back to study her map once more. One hundred and forty strokes. The exact number of roses embroidered on her sofa, the exact number of letters on the paint label, the exact number of dots on her apron. She remembered being teased for that apron, that sofa, the record player. No one else used them anymore, but they were hers.

*Far away have I strayed, far from those I knew*

She folded herself onto the sofa. Paint can, wash-stand, apron, record-player. Everything in the right corner. Afghan across the arm of the sofa, for the evening. The stack of books, for the afternoon. For now, the music. She closed her eyes. Perhaps today would be a day to go outside, if the clouds left the sun alone. The porch needed painting, perhaps with the leftover green paint.

*But I'm sure I will be coming home to you*

Still without looking, she shifted the needle to the final movement. The crescendo of strings and horns chased away her tranquility, and she opened her eyes to a blank wall.

"No," she whispered, her voice lost in the music's crescendo. "I'll simply paint it—again."

She almost fell from the sofa in her hurry to reach the paint, but both paint and brush had vanished. When she turned to silence the music, tried to think, a voice echoed in the hall outside.

"She's coming, but we'll have to take it slowly—it's been a long time."

The symphony ended, a last grand resolution. Intent on the voice, she only glanced at the empty corner where the record player had been.

"Easy now, not too quickly. Watch the monitor for stress. Steady, there we go."

She blinked, quickly but deliberately. Her apron and her stacks of books were no longer in their places. She realized she was sitting on the floor, without her sofa cushions. She fumbled for her afghan and draped it around her shoulders, shuddering.

"Slower, slower, or her signs will destabilize. Gently, please."

A sunbeam fell across her lap, and she stopped shivering. The afghan disappeared, but she smiled.

"There, that's it. Just a moment more."

She curled up on the floor. The voice was closer now, but company would have to let themselves in. She needed a quiet rest first, and then she would talk to her visitors. And paint the porch. And water her roses. How long had it been since she'd slept?

"Hello? Can you hear me? Can you try to speak?"

She opened her eyes. A man in a white coat was bending over her.

"Loretta, can you hear me?"

She tried to hum the last movement of the symphony, to clear the catch in her throat, but no sound came. Carefully, she nodded.

The doctor smiled. "Wonderful, just wonderful."

He pressed a switch, and she felt herself lifting. When she held out her hands, he pressed a glass of water into them. Tilting the glass, she drank. Raindrop blue. Over the doctor's shoulder, through the shimmering glass window, she saw a sweep of hills. Darkened green.

She glanced at the doctor, who was reading something from the tablet in his hands. "Are we home?"

"All vitals read normal," he said, lifting the empty glass from her hand. "Suspension was successful, Miss McRoy."

She nodded. "And the date?"

He shook his head. "2150, January 1st. We were unable to extend stasis for longer than expected."

Her breath caught like the silence at the end of her symphony. "My birthday," she whispered. "January 1, 1990." She sat in the silence for a moment, then she smiled. "Don't tell me how old I am, please."

"Of course not," he said, smiling in return. "But I can tell you anything else you want to know."

She tilted her head, imagining the feel of her paintbrush in her fingers. "Do people still listen to Dvořák's symphonies?"

He frowned. "I'm used to the music of these monitors—that's a question for James."

"James?" She glanced down at her dress, adjusting the one crooked button in the long row between her collar and her waistband.

The doctor grinned. "My colleague. He's developed quite the interest in Mozart since he learned about your brother Jacob's music. Developed quite an interest in history, too, especially because you happen to be—" He glanced down at his tablet, which had begun emitting a consistent crescendo of noise, and then back at her. "I have to go."

She exhaled slowly. "It's mother, isn't it? She's probably running late." When the doctor nodded, she added, "Of all of us, she would get—lost—the most often."

The doctor scanned her monitor, then turned to leave. "Try and get some sleep," he said. "I'll send James in to see you—he'll know more than I do about the things you want to know."

He lowered her bed, and she lay back against the regulation cushions. "James," she whispered. "At least they still have historical names in the 22nd century. Variant for Jacob, from the Hebrew—"

Her eyes closed. When she opened them again, another young doctor was standing half-turned towards her, scanning rapidly though a tablet. After a moment, she drew a breath and sat up, summoning a smile as hidden as Mona Lisa's.

"Well," she said, "as far as I can tell, we're home." He turned and stumbled over a monitor, but didn't answer. "Is that right, doctor?" she prompted. "Have we come out of suspension?" His mouth opened, but no words emerged.

She turned her head and glanced at her father and her brothers, all asleep. "Mother's running a little late. You'll try your best to wake her? I know there's some risk."

He nodded, and she let him see a hint more of the smile. "Do you have a name?" she asked, shaking her head when he glanced down at his identification badge. "There's another half, isn't there?"

He blushed. "Call me James."

She tilted her head to hide her laughter. "Because that's your name?"

"I'm Anderson," he finally stammered. "James Anderson."

### *Earth Setting*

My great-grandmother saw it first, back in the day when they still used Boeings for commercial travel. She'd been up in an airplane just once in her long life, and she told the story forever. The detail-loving grandkids contested that it didn't count, since it wasn't a view of the whole Earth, but she stuck to it anyway.

"Loretta," she'd say to me, and whoever else happened to be listening, "don't you know what it's like? Up in the sky, who knows how far from the ground, and suddenly you realize the earth isn't flat anymore." We'd heard this story a thousand times, but she'd keep going. "The curve of the earth, all blue and cloudy—"

"And those flat-earth people never had a chance!" we would all chorus along with her. But honestly, I didn't know what she meant until I saw it myself, from much further away. That's right, I became an astronaut. Grandmam was thrilled, of course.

"Loretta Anderson, astronaut," she said, before they shipped us out. "It's almost like I'll be in space myself!" I remember laughing with her about that—I guess having an old-fashioned name that matches your great-grandmother's has its eventual perks. Technically, I'm a panzoölogist with specializations in extraplanetary life forms and linguistics—an alien scientist—but astronaut works.

I really shouldn't have felt that odd about seeing Earth from so far away. After all, we'd done orientation excursions, learning how to operate a cruiser within safe bailing distance of Earth. Even specialists had to learn the basics—we'd be sitting weight for most of the trip otherwise—and I got used to passing by the blue-green-cloudy thing just hanging out there in orbit. I almost forgot how weird it was that I wasn't standing on Earth myself, that I wasn't moored securely on that small sphere we called home.

Then we got leveled up from orientation excursions, almost too quickly. My colleagues tossed around speculations that the higher-ups were shoving our expeditions through, and I almost agreed with them. Whatever the case, an avenue to an unexplored planet opened up, and our cruiser drew the lucky number. She has the latest in lightspeed function, and she could bypass most of the interstellar traffic without even registering on their sensors. Yeah, lightspeed is a thing now. The real 23rd century isn't a whole lot like *Star Trek,* but we do have that.

Anyway, we took *Lightfoot* out of Earth's orbit without touching the warp drive, so I saw it drop over the edge of the observation deck, almost like the sun setting. It's really just the way the deck is curved, but something went down when we lost sight of that blue smudge.

Even though we tracked it on our sensors, I went the next few shifts feeling like I'd come loose from something.

And then we hit warp drive, and I mostly forgot about it. You'd think a cruise into a different system would take forever, but we were on high warp most of the way, and monitoring *Lightfoot* took a fair amount of concentration. Not to mention that my panzoölogy books didn't need much reviewing. What's the good of cataloguing the 'basic life form' when they take all shapes and sizes? Whatever was on this planet didn't have to fit any of our boxes. So I spent most of the time serving as backup in the mechanical department. By the time we settled orbit on GT-937, I was seriously considering a second specialization in warp engineering.

But that's not as important. When we took our lifeboat down surface—that was something else.

Luckily, GT-937 supports human breathing and optimal function and all that. Even the gravity's not bad. When we took the lifeboat down, it actually stayed down, and we didn't need the support system for long at all. I guess we should stop calling our shuttles lifeboats, at least on planets like these. And gosh, this planet! It's reddish, like Mars, and it's got polar ice caps, like Mars, but the strangest thing is the light.

Yeah, the light. Ask the heliologists about this one, but whatever sun supports this planet emits way more light than our sun does. Apparently it's not high on the harmful ray scale, which I find a bit hard to believe, but it means that everything reflects just a tad more light than it would on Earth. It also means that the inhabitants of this planet—yes, it is inhabited—are a bit hard to catalogue. Maybe it's the exposure to all that light, something in their biological makeup, but they actually emit light. To this day, I'm still not sure whether they're humanoid or not, all because of the light. Either way—and this is where things got *really* interesting.

We don't have a universal translator—a *Star Trek* gadget I wish was real—but I was able to piece together a substantial vocabulary. They're not afraid of us, so I started with names. They can't pronounce the first syllable in 'Loretta' for some reason, so they just call me 'Etta.' I get the sense that they still laugh at me, but I don't mind. Eventually, I realized that the light they emit actually changes based on their emotions. When they're happy, they emit more light, and when they're upset or angry, they cloud over or lose the light altogether. We 'strange ship' people don't do this, and I think it confuses them that our states of mind aren't that clear. I guess they're simpler, more trusting than we are, and maybe that's not a bad thing.

One night, I was talking to one of them. She's called P'mëa, and boy is she opinionated. I was trying to convince her that it's okay to tell fiction stories, that people write fiction to try to make the world a little brighter, and she wasn't really buying it. They're all very literal when it comes to words, and she didn't like the idea of making things up. I appreciate her stubbornness and her honesty, but I was hoping she would at least give fiction a little space.

Then I was telling her about sunsets, and something clicked. She decided she could tell stories about my "staying-place," even if our sunrises and sunsets are the reverse of hers. The stars were out by this time, and I watched them with her for a while. We can't see Earth from here, of course, but I know the general direction. And, after the longest time of not thinking about home at all, I was suddenly thinking about Earth.

"Up there," I told P'mëa, "so far that the light does not reach, is my staying-place."

"What is your staying-place like?" she asked, brightening up like she does when she's curious.

They all think in terms of simple things, in terms of light and water, especially P'mëa. So I had to hunt around for the right words. "Blue, like much water gathered together to drink."

Their water is ice a lot of the time, so she got even brighter. "All your staying place is like that?"

"Except where the growing is, then it is green." I could tell this was a stumper for her. Green isn't really on their spectrum, so I said, "And there is my mother's mother's mother, Grandmam Etta. She is waiting to hear my stories of what is, about you and your staying-place."

Her light got softer. "She must have much light, if she has that many years."

I smiled past the catch in my voice. "Yes, much light. She was first of us to see the Earth-setting."

## Sun Setting

She remembered the ebb and flow of the light, her words measured as drops of water on rock. And then she spoke.

"One day, the sun rose in the west and set in the east—"

She saw the Teacher move, a flash of light that hurt her eyes and caught her breath. Her tale ended, the rush of a stream, and she did not hear the tales the others told. Then they went away. She waited, her light fading, for the Teacher.

"You must learn to do better, P'mëa," he said. "Did you not hear the others?"

"Yes, Teacher," she said, softly. "But I remembered the light, did I not?"

"That is not everything." The Teacher looked at her, the thunder in his eyes a little less. "The tales of the others, did you not hear?"

"I do not understand," she whispered. "How can we make tales of what is not? Are not tales told of what is?"

The Teacher shone a little brighter. "Yes, P'mëa, but you must also learn to make tales of things that are not."

"Why?" She knew her light was a fading sunset, covered in clouds, but she could not change it.

The Teacher's light dimmed, only for a moment. "The others who have come make stories of things that are not. We try to learn their ways, to tell their tales."

She was all darkness now, without stars. "I do not like their ways. They are like water run dry."

The Teacher said nothing. She turned away, and saw K'tor was waiting for her. Her light leapt up again, and they went away together.

"Why do you question the Teacher?" he asked. "It is not right to question, P'mëa."

Her darkness fell again. "My tale was a good tale," she said. "It was a right tale."

He laughed, like a new rain. "But our sun climbs west and falls east every day. The Teacher did not want that old tale. The tales of the others who have come—"

"I do not want to be like them, K'tor. They do not have light like ours, and they make tales of what is not. How is that right?" She looked at him, and his light dimmed as the Teacher's.

"I do not know." His words were slow, like the words of tales. "They want to learn our ways. It is only right that we learn their ways."

"Is it right? I do not think so." She looked to the setting sun, and her long shadow.

K'tor smiled, like the air after rain. "You think many things, P'mëa. You are not always right."

He went his own way, his shadow crossing hers and winding away like a dark snake. She watched him until his light almost joined with the sun.

"It's beautiful, isn't it?"

She turned. One of the others stood there, the others who had no light.

"Etta," she said, slowly. "She of the strange ships, I do not understand this 'beautiful.'"

Etta smiled, and there was some light in it. "Your way of words is—strange—to me. Let me think how to tell of 'beautiful.'" She sat down on a white stone, that long ago would have flown with water, and she spoke to herself in her own words.

P'mëa did not understand, but she looked again at this one of the others, this one who came in the ships and spoke to them, who asked them of their ways and learned their way of words. The one who was not like them, but the one who held light in her smile.

"Beautiful," Etta said, carefully, "is the sky when the sun falls. It is the rain that comes after a long time. It is a tale that does not grow old for the telling."

P'mëa felt her light grow and fade, a flash in a storm. "But your tales are not beautiful. Our tales speak of the sun and the rain, as they are."

Etta laughed. "You like the sun and the rain, P'mëa. So do I. So does everyone, other or not."

"I do not like your tales," she said, but she felt her light growing still. "You make tales of what is not, and tales must be of what is. Light on sun, and light on water, and light on stone—these are tales of what is."

Etta nodded. "Tales of what is, they are good tales. But also the tales of what are not." She looked out at the sun, fallen far now, and back to P'mëa. "If I told a tale of you, a tale of what is, to those in my staying-place—my home—they would say I told of what is not."

She did not look at Etta. "But I am here, Etta. And they would call me what is not?" The sun fell, and her light dimmed.

"They would not understand that you are here. We make many tales of what is not, P'mëa. Our staying-place is small, and we have little light. So we make our tales."

"A tale of what is not that gives light," she said, the lightest breath.

"Your tales of what is, they are full of light to us," Etta said, her words a hurrying stream. "Your sun, falling east and rising west, is a light, because our sun is not like this. In my home, we say, 'One day, the sun rose in the east and fell in the west,' and that is what is."

She looked at Etta, her light like the hidden stars. "But your sun is a tale of what is not!"

Etta smiled. "For us, a tale of what is."

For a long time, she did not speak. The clouds fell away above them, and the stars shone down on the white stone, on Etta, and on her. "And your tale, this tale of what is—this is beautiful?"

"Our tale, and yours," Etta said, and her light shone, "they are both beautiful."

She remembered drops of water on rock, the ebb and flow of the light. "Then, I will begin my tale like this. One day, the sun rose in the east and set in the west, and it was—beautiful."

## Essential Threesome

*November 28, 2220*

"Do I look like the kind of person who would start a galactic-scale war?" I asked. "A whole war, even if we are only in a simulator?"

The Commander just smiled at me, the all-knowing look which I knew too well.

"Just because I watch *Star Trek* doesn't mean I'm deranged!" I protested. "Their fictionalized technology was outdated long ago."

"Listen, Sam." The tone was supposed to calm me, but I don't think it worked. "What do you think the purpose of training is? Ground for indulging your personal fantasies?"

"No, Commander," I said. "That would be illogical."

He slammed his fist on the console, and a dozen lights blinked. "Dash it all, Sam!" he shouted. "When will this nonsense stop?"

I punched buttons rapid-fire until the lights stabilized. "Look, Commander," I said, taking a deep breath, "I'm one of the best trainees on this cruiser, and you know it. Physicals, emergency response time, initiative—everything is above normal."

"Except your psychological state," he said dryly. "I call that into serious question, Cadet Robinson."

"But unless you grant me room to maneuver, you're going to lose this top cadet," I said. "A bit of eccentricity keeps me sane."

He looked away, and I sensed the battle was won. "Carry on, Robinson. But if this interferes with execution of your duties—"

"It won't, Commander," I said. "It never has."

Okay, that's not strictly true. I just put that little exchange at the beginning to show you what life is like as a cadet-in-training, and I won't deny that my little daydreams have, on rare occasions, proved a fascinating distraction. And there it goes again, that *fascinating*. Double-triple drat—the head of the threesome's coming out exactly when I don't need him.

They don't consider themselves multiple personalities—I just have a unique mental processing mechanism. Honest, Grandmam, don't worry. After all, you were the one who introduced me to the original threesome in the first place, and you're never wrong about anything. Just don't let anyone else read this, all right? Not even Grandpap.

If you really want to know, the Commander did actually get angry at me for setting up a war situation in our simulator that day, and I did a poor job of deflecting the blame on the computer programming. I'm not an expert with the simulator, but I know how to configure basic scenarios, and the Commander didn't want me programming for battle. He thinks that, since we're going to GT-937, we don't need to practice war against the life forms there. I'm sure they're peaceful, because Loretta says so, but that doesn't mean we won't meet other hostile life forms in transit.

Anyway, I'm not in disgrace. As I told the Commander, my record's too good to lose, and maybe having Loretta for a cousin does something too. It's not logical, this family preference in the program, but it has advantages. Can you tell the Vulcan side is coming out? But the fact that I'm okay with this preference at all, that's the doctor's side. Oh, and here comes the captain, telling them politely to shut up and get on with their duties, which is really what I should be doing. I'm back on helm control in a minute—stay tuned for the next installment!

*December 14, 2220*

Well, I'm scribbling this in the infirmary, hoping the attendants won't see. Of the threesome running around in my consciousness, I think the Vulcan feels most vindicated at the moment. We did in fact encounter some of what the Commander calls 'interference' from some unidentified life-forms, landing a good number of the crew in the aforementioned infirmary. If we'd trained for it, according to the proper procedures—but I don't want to diminish the Commander's efforts. I'm trying to convince myself that we all did the best we could.

Don't worry—I'm completely fine, but I did earn myself a nasty knock on the head, and I think it's made the threesome unhappy. While the Vulcan, for instance, is quite pleased that his deductions were obviously correct, the doctor's upset that the life-forms attacked at all, and the captain's having a rough time keeping peace. Listen:

"They attacked a ship full of trainees! Not even a heartless, green-blooded alien would do that."

"Such a course of action would be infallibly illogical, doctor, only if these life-forms were not hostile to us. It appears, according to all available data, that they were in fact hostile."

"I don't need you to point out the obvious! Untried young hands fighting their own adrenaline to try and save a ship less fit for space than my uncle's antique automobile—why, the situation's practically inviting panic."

"Whether or not this cruiser is space-worthy is a matter for the engineering department. The unfortunate presence of adrenaline in humans, however, does not excuse the conduct of Cadet Robinson."

"Oh, really? If the kid gets a bit wild and pulls the helm away a few degrees to avoid enemy fire, wouldn't any other trainee in the same boat forget that other ship turns faster?"

"Given supporting evidence, it is a puzzling error on the cadet's part, but an error nonetheless."

"Well, least it's not *illogical*, or *fascinating*, or even *interesting*. The kid's got a bump that would put any cadet out of commission for weeks. What would you call that?"

"Now, gentlemen, please. The cadet failed to follow orders precisely, and a proper demand will be given. But the attempt to prevent damage to the vessel did end with some degree of success. I think we'll consider discussion at an end."

You see? That's what it's been like for days now, inside my head. The captain usually chimes in at the end with a balanced assessment of the situation, but the other two are having a fine time. Even the snippet of conversation above would tell you that I made a bit of a mistake, but imagine this conversation running constantly. At least they don't bother me when I sleep, which is plenty.

*December 20, 2220*

The Commander came to see me today, an interview which wasn't as terrible as I thought.

"Sam," he said, "please tell me you weren't daydreaming when the interference surfaced."

I shook my head—carefully, so as not to disturb the injury—and said, "No, I don't think I was. All three of them were reasonably quiet, and I was focused on the helm."

"But the error was still yours," he pointed out, gently enough.

"Yes, sir, I admit that. I'll remember to adjust my calculations for the next encounter."

He smiled a little, so I figured I wasn't in scorching trouble. "I think I'll do the adjusting, and you'll make sure to follow orders to the letter. Fair?"

"Of course, Commander. You're never anything except fair."

At this point, I was doing my best not to smile, but I don't think he noticed. Starting today, I'm officially out of the infirmary, and I think I'll go back on duty soon. Oddly enough, the threesome is strangely quiet today.

*December 24, 2220*

Merry Christmas to the world's best Grandmam! I'm going to punch this in, encrypt it, and send it on its electronic way today. We're orbiting GT-937 now, but we can still make these long-distance transmissions from the cruiser. I'm sending this before we go down surface to celebrate with Loretta. I don't think the life forms she's befriended have this holiday, but we'll have an illuminating cultural exchange all the same.

Does the Vulcan say *illuminating*? I can't remember. He's been strangely quiet since the Commander came to see me. Maybe he's in awe of the Commander's logic, or something. The doctor's happy we're having warm feelings and hot cider (or at least the GT-937 equivalent). I'm sure the captain's just happy not to arbitrate their disputes for a day or two. And Cadet Sam Robinson's more or less back at the helm of the ship inside the head. So, everyone's happy.

*Postscript*

The Commander's just been in, a lightning strike visit. He's wondering what you would like for Christmas. If you send a reply soon, he might get it to you by New Year's, via prearranged Earth-bound transport (I know you don't trust those, but he'll be happy if you humor him).

"You have a wonderful great-grandmother," he said, halfway out the door. "Don't forget that."

As if he has to remind me. "Sure, Dad," I said. "I don't think I've ever forgotten."

And the threesome didn't say anything—it was all-genuine Sam. What do you think of that?

*Traveling to Infinity*

"Look, you don't have to take me seriously, but I think I'm becoming one of them."

She hardly glanced up from her notes, a deliberate choice of old-fashioned pen and paper, when Sam made his dramatic entrance.

"Scientifically speaking, I'm not sure that's possible," she said, her brain tapping into the stock replies reserved for her imaginative cousin.

"Come on, Loretta! At least run a bio scan first, and then use all the science lines you want."

His unspoken *please* caught her attention, so she settled her pen behind her ear. Sam dropped into the folding chair opposite hers and held out his empty hands.

"Well, I can tell you haven't been disturbing the planet's surface with a shovel recently—no reddish soil stains." She squinted slightly and grinned. "Maybe a slight sunburn, but I don't see what else is wrong with you."

"Don't you have one of those scanners from the bio department?" He glanced around the tent, watching the canvas walls snap in the breeze. "You borrowed one to test them, didn't you?"

"I wish you wouldn't refer to the Lucians as 'them' all the time." She tried not to sound like a nagging older sister, but Sam's face told her it probably came across that way.

"Well, why did you name them the Lucians? *Phototropons* would have been just as nerdy."

She reached for the bio scanner and ran a non-contact sequence. "*Lucis* for *of light* is less accurate than *phototropos* for *light-turner*. But it's Latin over Greek, and you don't really care either way."

He almost smiled, then winced as she initiated the contact sequence. The bio scanner beeped acknowledgement after extracting a sample from his thumb, settling into a quiet whir as the information processed.

"And I didn't really name the Lucians. They have a name already, but it's highly sacred and massively unpronounceable." She couldn't help chuckling, and he laughed along with her.

"Yeah, I tried to get K'tor to tell me what it was the other day, and he went dark as a stellar stormcloud." He stared at the pinprick in his thumb as the scanner initiated cellular repair. "Well, Doc, what's the diagnosis?"

She frowned at the scanner, a clunky rectangle not much bigger than an antique iPhone, and squinted as the pixels hinted that they might start to coalesce on the screen.

"You'd think our interface would be seamless," Sam commented, "but when it comes to these scanners—hey, Loretta? I'm still bleeding."

She stared at Sam's hand. The cut wasn't gushing—the scanner had taken a minuscule sample—but droplets were still trickling down his thumb.

She frowned. "Cellular repair should have reached completion almost immediately."

The bio scanner beeped again, signaling a completed analysis. Sam pressed his thumb to the edge of his uniform and bent over the screen. He finished reading before she did, but he shrugged.

"I'm just the tech guy, not the scientist," he announced, "no good with biological formulas."

"Formulae," she corrected, automatically taking Sam down a small notch. Because the Latin—"

Her reply shut off abruptly as the information on the screen claimed her full attention. A crowd of exhilarated Lucian children flashed by the tent like a collection of supernovas, momentarily blinding her.

"Hey, school's out," Sam said. "I guess some things are the same across planets."

She took a deep breath. "Sam, I think we'll have to run this sample up to *Lightfoot*. The scanner's not giving an accurate read, and I might need you for another sample."

Sam shook his head. "I know the operating system on those, and the scanner should read accurately. Do I have to call the Commander on you?"

"No, don't drag Uncle Rob into this yet." She swallowed hard. "The way these readings are, it looks like you were right after all."

He studied his thumb and then grinned at her. "When I said I was a tech guy, I didn't mean I couldn't take simple science. My gut feeling was right because—"

She let the silence sit between them for a moment, and then filled it. "Because you're altering at the cellular level. The element that allows the Lucians to produce their light—it's taking over your cells. The rate it's going, you'll start glowing soon. Or not, if you're unhappy."

Sam tried to whistle, and she laughed shakily at his failure. "Well, the doctor in my head was right about the feeling," he said. "And the Vulcan tried denying it—not logical and all that."

"Well, it isn't logical," she admitted. "I've been here much longer than you have, and I've never felt—how exactly are you feeling?"

"Like I have a fever," he answered promptly, "but I know I don't have one."

She retrieved her pen and scratched a few words on the paper. "I think we'll have to run you up to *Lightfoot* after all and confirm that."

He picked up her pen and rolled it between his fingers. "Does the Commander have to know?"

Through the tent flap, she watched the sun drop into the east. "Sam, why wouldn't you want him to know?"

The pen rolled too quickly, and he almost tipped out of his chair to pick it up. "The training cruiser is leaving soon, and I want one of the assignments here. GT-937 doesn't have much in the way of tech, but I'd still like to stay. If Dad finds out—"

"He'll take you to the nearest medical station," she interrupted, "and why shouldn't he?"

Before he could reply, a muted flash—the signal of an approaching Lucian—startled them both.

"K'tor, why have you come here?" She stumbled over the name that had given her no trouble for months, but spoke the Lucian words without thinking.

"Looking for Sam," he said, his light flaring as he struggled over the beginning of the name. "Is he not to go with me today? I have shown him places of water, places of light. There are more."

"Did P'mëa not show these places to me?" she asked. "What places did you show Sam?"

"The staying-place of the light, what you call *home*," K'tor said, his light dimming. "P'mëa has not seen this. I did not show her, but I showed Sam. Please, do not speak hard words."

She held her hands out, palms up, in the gesture of peace. "I will not speak hard words. But, K'tor, the staying-place of the light is not for ship people. Sam's light is—dark."

"But the light is beginning in him," K'tor said, his own light almost fading. "Of all the ship people, there is light in him."

Sam held out his hands. "It may be dark for me, K'tor," he said clumsily. "Loretta and I must go to our ship and see."

"But light is not danger," K'tor insisted. His somber glow fell across Sam's hands.

"For the ship people, it may be," Sam said. "Our ship will tell us."

K'tor didn't answer, but his light faded completely, and he left the tent.

"His light is like one of Grandmam's old theaters," Sam whispered. "When the lights go down—" He stopped. "Never mind. I suppose my lights could be going down, couldn't they?"

"Leave the metaphors to the linguists, Sam," she managed. "Let's find the Commander and ask permission to visit *Lightfoot*."

Sam nodded, but neither of them moved. Suddenly, he grinned. "Hey, the doctor says turning into a Lucian would be a great medical discovery."

She couldn't help the smallest of smiles. "And I suppose the Vulcan thinks it's illogical?"

Sam stood up and held back the tent flap. "No, he's sure it's *fascinating*. Whatever happens, they're actually agreeing for once. Just wait till Grandmam hears about this!"

"Put the brakes on that cruiser inside your head, Sam," she said, teasing by default, "at least until we've solved this mystery."

****

The full-body scanner signaled the end of its contact sequence, breaking the comfortable rhythm of noises on a cruiser at rest.

"Why do they make these so obnoxious?" she muttered, flipping the switch to initiate Sam's emergence from the scanner.

While she waited for the readout to load on her screen, she studied Sam. Underneath the scanner's transparent dome, he was inexplicably smiling. When the dome lifted, he opened his eyes and pantomimed exaggerated drinking motions.

"All right, jokester," she said. "Just wait for the readout, then you can have the filtered stuff."

Except for the whirring scanner, the noise in the infirmary subsided. She could feel the faint rumble of the engines through her feet, hear the crackle as someone opened an intercom accidentally.

She glanced at the scanner screen, which was still loading data, and then turned to fill a cup for Sam. "Six ounces of dihydrogen monoxide, filtered," she announced.

He pushed himself into a sitting position and accepted the cup. "Water, you mean," he said, his voice cracking. "What is it about the scanner that makes me so disoriented?"

"Maybe your overactive imagination affects your nervous system," she suggested, refilling the cup. "The department doesn't have to sedate many people for a scan, after all."

He shook the last drops into his mouth. "Every time a take a trip in that thing, I come out feeling like my head's been drained of everything useful."

"Blame the sedation for that," she suggested. "At least the fellows in your head will give you a moment's peace."

He grinned crookedly. "The Vulcan's logic and the doctor's emotion are equally squashed. There's no peace for the captain to keep this time." As he dropped back against the scanner's flatbed, he added, "Can I have some more dihydrogen monoxide?"

The scanner signaled report completion, and she scrolled through for abnormal data. "Shouldn't have too much, Sam, or your system will overload. You already have—"

"Really," he interrupted, "I feel like I'm overloading from the inside. If I had water, maybe we could douse the fire."

She adjusted the scanner's monitor and skipped back two screens. "I think we're going to need a lot more than water, Sam."

She tried to keep her voice steady, and Sam tried to smile. "Hey, it can't be that bad. A fever's not going to kill—"

"Oh, shut up," she said, reaching deep into her uniform pocket for her pen. "Just shut up."

Sam slid off the table. "All right, Loretta lump-head," he whispered. "I won't make jokes."

His fingers just brushed the elbow of her borrowed lab coat. For a moment, she felt as if the fabric had been instant-dried, but the heat faded. Then Sam leaned against the edge of the flatbed, almost falling over when it started to roll away from him.

She dropped her pen back into her pocket and reached out to stop the flight of the flatbed. "The scanner's confirmed that your cells are altering. That light-producing element isn't a problem for Lucians, but it's literally turning up the heat in your cells."

"So I'm going to burn up?" Sam glanced away as if he didn't expect an answer.

She started to reply when the intercom crackled. After a moment, she rerouted the intercom through the scanner and pushed a button. The Commander's face, still slightly pixelated, flashed onto the screen.

"Cadet Robinson, I don't suppose this will stop you from embarking on expeditions with the native population," he said.

Sam shook his head. "Sorry, sir. In my defense, we didn't realize that this element existed, or that exposure would have potentially lethal consequences."

"Suggested treatment, Officer Anderson?" A flash of light momentarily distorted his face.

"That would be up to the medical department, sir. Panzoölogists aren't qualified—"

"I asked for suggestions, Anderson." The light faded, and the Commander's face reappeared.

She took a deep breath. "In order to counteract the element pervading the cadet's system, we could expose him to an element on the extreme opposite end of the spectrum."

Sam laughed. "What, put me on ice like they did to Cap in those old movies?"

She couldn't help smiling. "That might keep your temperature down, but exposure to a corresponding Lucian element, some kind of anti-light principle, could potentially return your cells to their original state."

The Commander nodded. "Thank you, Loretta."

She executed her most precise salute. "You're welcome, Uncle Rob."

"See, Dad?" Sam added. "I told you she'd have an answer somewhere."

The Commander returned her salute. "I knew she would, Sam. Commander out." His image faded. The intercom static lasted a second longer, but the scanner shifted to standby.

Sam heaved himself onto the flatbed, sandwiching his hands between his head and the pillow. "You're sure the Lucians have a 'corresponding element,' aren't you?"

She wheeled the flatbed into the smallest infirmary compartment and turned down the room controls. "No," she admitted, "but it's logical."

"Oh, the Vulcan's disagreeing with you," he said. "You don't have enough data to draw a conclusion."

She shivered as the temperature hit a low point. "Okay, let's get some data. K'tor took you to the home of the light, probably one of the Lucian sacred places."

"Yeah, it was underground somewhere, around their equator." His fever-induced flush faded slightly. "He took me plenty of places, except the ice caps."

She felt his forehead. "The ice caps? P'mëa told me that the Lucians who bring their water from the ice caps don't shine as brightly."

"There's the data!" Sam announced, swatting away her hand. "If there's a light-dampening element somewhere, it'll be at the ice caps."

"Maybe that isn't enough data," she said. "Your fever's gone down, but it's still a risk."

"Forget the Vulcan," Sam said. "I don't want to spend the rest of my existence in a temperature- controlled cell, and the doctor's ready to take a risk. If it's a choice between burn up or freeze—"

"You'd rather freeze." She matched her breathing to the rumble of the engines. "What's the captain say?"

Sam smiled. "Whatever it takes to keep this ship running, he's willing to try."

She reached for her pen again, inspecting the pocket for accidental ink stains. "And what does Sam say?"

Sam frowned for a moment, and then his expression cleared. "He agrees with the captain on this one. What's your opinion, Officer Anderson?"

She almost laughed. "Now you sound like Uncle Rob." The intercom in their compartment crackled, and she spoke into it. "This is Officer Anderson, from the infirmary. There's an open intercom circuit—"

"Loretta, it's Uncle Rob. I'm on an individual relay circuit. Is Sam with you?"

She nodded, forgetting that he couldn't see her. "Yes, sir. Is there a problem?"

For a moment, she thought the relay was broken, but the Commander answered. "I've just spoken to that Lucian friend of Sam's about your theory. From what I understood, he didn't like the idea of cellular change."

She glanced at Sam, who was frowning again. "He didn't think it would work?"

"No, but he said something about 'hardened water' that put his light out. Could you come down surface and talk to him?"

"As long as I can come," Sam said, his frown disappearing. "I could convince K'tor—"

"You need to stay here and keep your fever down," she said, bringing out her 'nagging older sister voice' in spite of Sam's silent pleas.

"Bring the cadet with you, Anderson," the Commander interrupted. "Double time, please."

She sighed, remembering too late that the intercom was still open. "Yes, sir. Anderson out."

When she closed the intercom, Sam returned to his frown. "He was worried. He never uses our names like that unless we're in unusual situations."

"I'd call this an unusual situation, wouldn't you?" She adjusted the compartment temperature to normal levels and added softly, "We're all worried, Sam."

"K'tor too," he agreed, glancing quickly at her. "I wonder what's so terrible about your theory?"

She tried to smile, but from Sam's reaction, she guessed the smile ended in a grimace. "I don't know, but K'tor does. Whatever hint of danger turned out his light, we'll find it."

****

*It's so cold. Why did he bring me down here? The light's going out, mind and his. So cold, the light in me is gone. All on fire, but now—*

Sam tore the piece of paper from her hands. "This isn't your usual letter to Grandmam, is it?" she asked, already sure of the answer.

He clenched his fists, wrinkling the paper like an ancient parchment. "I tried making it a story. You know, a dramatic first-person thing?"

She couldn't help grinning. "Well, it sounds like an angsty teen novel from the 2000s, maybe the 2010s. I'd stick with the letters to Grandmam."

He frowned. "Leave stories to the linguists, right?"

Sliding the bio scanner from the pocket of her lab coat, she ran a contact temperature check on her cousin. "No, not always," she admitted. "It's just not like you to be dramatic."

The bio scanner signaled completion, and Sam settled back into his seat. "Fair observation," he said, adjusting the harnesses that held them securely in their automated lifeboat. "If I could borrow your pen, I'll attempt something else."

She reached into her pocket. "Well, since you already borrowed that page from my notebook, and as long as this is the only page, you can."

"It was from the back, I promise," he said, commencing a new round of scribbling.

While he scribbled, she logged his temperature readings. The red line on the instant chart inched up a fraction just as the lifeboat grounded, but Sam only glanced up when the dome of the lifeboat lifted. Together, they untangled their harnesses and stepped out.

"Exit complete," she announced to the empty lifeboat. "Initiate automated return."

The dome snapped back into place, and they braced themselves against the engine draft as the lifeboat achieved liftoff. Once their craft was clearly on route to *Lightfoot*, Sam held out the paper.

*Do you know how it feels to burn? Not a laser burn, or an electric burn, or even an old-fashioned stove burn, but burning up from the inside? You're so hot that machines can't hold you, but you don't notice. You're sure it'll be a long time before—*

"I decided to try second person," Sam broke in. "Sounds more like me, but a little forced."

She tried to laugh. "A bit too real, Sam. You really are burning up, and if we can't get you to those ice caps—"

"Cadet Robinson, Officer Anderson! Over here, please."

They turned, saluting simultaneously. The Commander stood several paces away, K'tor next to him. When Sam ran to them, she followed carefully. The Lucian's light dimmed and flashed so quickly that her eyes ached, but she could still understand his speech.

"If you take Sam to the place of hardened water, his light will go out forever," K'tor insisted. "There is no light there. There is something there that makes light dark forever."

The Commander shook his head. "I can't follow him, Loretta. Whenever I asked him to speak slowly, he only spoke faster."

She reached out to K'tor, her palms up. "Calm your light, K'tor," she said gently. "Tell me again what you told the Commander."

Sam caught his breath. "Hey, Loretta, I can see him. Really see him, in all the light. Definitely humanoid."

She shook her head. "Now's not the time for scientific discoveries, Sam. Tell me again, K'tor."

K'tor's light settled. "If you take Sam where you wish to take him, he will—die. That is what you call going out forever."

"But only Lucians who stay in the darkest places die," Sam said. "I'm not a Lucian, K'tor."

"You are more of us than of them, now," K'tor answered, his light flaring. "Soon, they will be able to see the light I see in you."

"And by that point?" the Commander asked, holding out his hand for the bio scanner.

"By that point," she said, almost whispering, "he'll be dead. Look at his temperature now."

She turned away and realized that Sam was scribbling again. "How's this?" he said. "A little artistic license this time."

*"Well, we finally found him out."*

*"Oh, really? What did he have planned this time?"*

*"He was going to blow the whole place up, can you believe that?"*

*"He's certainly got the gumption, that's for sure."*

*"Yeah, but only half the smarts. He was going to use—"*

She laughed shakily. "I suppose you're the thing he was planning to blow up?"

He nodded. "It was a bit weird, calling the Lucian-morphing cells *he* instead of *they* So definitely license, but—hey, the lifeboat's coming back."

The Commander handed back the bio scanner. "Yes it is, Cadet Robinson. If we're going to reach the ice caps in time, we need transport."

She glanced from K'tor to Sam. "You're taking him to the ice caps? Isn't there a risk, if he's becoming Lucian?"

The Commander hesitated for the smallest moment, but Sam spoke up. "If we don't get me there, I'm going down anyway," he said simply.

She watched the lifeboat, the size of a small cloud, circle back to them. Once it grounded, Sam and the Commander marched off in true cadet step, but she glanced at K'tor.

"You are taking Sam to the hardened water," the Lucian sad, his light fading.

She nodded. "We must. If we do, or if we do not, his light may still go out forever."

"You must try," he said, a blinding flash. "I cannot come in your ship, but I will go to the place of hardened water and wait for you."

She nodded again. For a moment, the Lucian's brightness blurred. "Thank you, K'tor."

As she ran for the lifeboat, she glanced over her shoulder at K'tor, who was streaking away like a star. The dome settled and harnesses dropped into place, but she could still see him. Even after the lifeboat reached liftoff, low-altitude navigation kept him in range.

Sam tapped her shoulder. "You don't have to watch him from the windows, Loretta. Dad's piloting, and he's got the appropriate scanners set to detect a Lucian at high speeds."

She reached for his hand. "I know, but I—Sam, your hand is glowing now."

He studied his fingers, then rolled up the sleeve of his uniform. "It's not just my hand, either. Fascinating."

"Oh, the Vulcan's finally decided to come out?" she said. "I suppose this is science."

"A test," Sam announced. "Lucian expert, read my light. Feelings?"

She took a deep breath and tried to smile. "Not enough light to tell for sure, but I'd say excited, or anticipating something."

Sam grinned. "The doctor says my feelings have been correctly diagnosed, but the Vulcan—"

"Well, as long as the doctor agrees with me, the Vulcan doesn't matter," she interrupted.

Sam stared at her. "Afraid of what logic will tell you?" he asked.

She nodded and glanced out the window. The ice caps rushed nearer, and K'tor's light blended with them until she could no longer see him.

"So am I," he whispered. "Just an atom or two of fear, that's all." He held out the creased piece of paper. "Here, read this."

*Here's how the story ends: We'll head down into the hidden places beneath the ice caps. Loretta and Dad will be cold, K'tor won't be the brightest. but I'll be fine. Sooner or later, I'll stop burning. We won't be there long enough to freeze Dad, or Loretta, or K'tor. K'tor will probably try to be a hero, but I'll make sure he comes out bright. What else are friends for? I've never tried writing a story that wasn't in a letter to Grandmam, but this is how this one will end.*

She looked up and smiled. "You're sure about this, aren't you?"

He mirrored her smile. "Very sure. It's time this story came to an end."

****

"Loretta, isn't it time for those temperature checks Dad wants?" Sam shook her by both shoulders of her multipurpose suit. "Loretta? Where's the scanner?"

The glinting walls that surrounded them crowded into her vision until she could almost feel the points of ice. When she tried to turn her head, she couldn't look at her cousin.

"The inner pocket," she managed. "Be careful. Temperature may have damaged it."

Sam fumbled for the scanner, and she heard the crinkle of chemically-engineered insulation. Sam's suit-to-suit communication clicked off, and he removed his helmet to run the scan. Her visor blurred the numbers, but she watched the red line drop.

"It's working, Uncle Rob," she whispered. "His temperature's coming down. But I can't move very easily. Can you?"

Static crackled in her ears, and the Commander's voice sounded. "No. It must be the cold. Our suits can't withstand it."

Automatically, she started to look over her shoulder, but she couldn't complete the turn. Sam stood directly in her line of sight, holding the scanner in his faintly glowing hands.

"I'll have to wait here." The Commander's voice faded to a whisper. "I'll try and contact the officers waiting above the surface."

Sam lowered his helmet, and a clearer voice sounded over the static. "Loretta? My temperature's down to normal. Is K'tor still with Dad?"

She tried to shake her head, but the cold forestalled her. "I don't know. Can you see him?"

Sam replaced the scanner and looked past her, over her shoulder. "Yeah. His light's way back there. He's unhappy, or in danger, because it's not very bright. And I can see a dark smudge, probably Dad."

"But our suits are white," she objected. "Those Lucian cells must be getting to you."

He grinned. "I guess they see things differently—but at least I'm not burning up from the inside." His gaze shifted over her shoulder again, and she watched his smile fade.

"Are they far behind?" she prompted. "He said we might have to leave him."

He nodded. "K'tor's light is getting dimmer, too. We should have made them stay."

Her laugh probably sounded more like a gasp. "He's the Commander, Sam. What could an officer and a cadet order him to do?"

Sam kicked at the ice crystals underfoot and almost slipped. "K'tor told me where to go. They didn't have to come."

"Suit-to-suit communication is not closed circuit, Cadet Robinson," the Commander interrupted. "I appreciate your concern, but you must go on. K'tor and I will remain here, or, if we can, join Officer Anderson."

She leaned against Sam and shuffled forward. "Uncle Rob, I can still walk. Can't I go with Sam?" For a moment, she listened to silence. "Commander? Commander? Come in, please."

Something that might have been a sigh cut across the static. "Yes, Commander coming in. The temperature's only going to drop from here, is that right?"

"Yes, sir," Sam said. "K'tor told me Lucians don't even go to the deepest places."

"Did he inform you have much further until cellular transformation takes place?"

"That's not a guarantee, sir." Loretta spoke before Sam could. "I know the risk for both of us."

The static increased, and then cleared as the Commander spoke. "I've connected to the officers on the surface of the planet, so I won't order you to stay."

She could almost hear Sam's smile. "Thanks, Dad. I didn't want to go alone."

"Take all due precaution, Loretta." The Commander's static completely disappeared. "You too, Sam. Don't let the doctor run this expedition."

Sam saluted. "Yes, sir. Loretta's running this one, and she's a scientist."

The Commander chuckled. "That's enough, Cadet. The surface is cutting in, so I'll sign off for a moment. Status updates, highest frequency."

Loretta released the breath she'd been holding. "Of course, sir." Another click sounded in her ears as the Commander switched communication circuits, then Sam's voice.

"Hey, Loretta? I have an idea. Could you slide off your gloves for a second?"

"And watch my fingers turn to ice?" She laughed. "The doctor must be talking."

He made a face. "No, it's the Vulcan and his logic. You saw me take off the helmet, right? I'm not even cold. My insulation is damp with—"

"Okay, I don't need to know the inner condition of your suit." She paused. "When I was testing you aboard *Lightfoot*, you were literally hot to the touch. Do you think you could—"

"Exactly," he said. "My temperature's not where it was then, but transfer is still possible."

"If you're wrong," she said, sliding off her gloves and grabbing Sam's hands, "I'll never— wait, I can move my fingers."

Sam nodded. "Makes me wonder what I could do. Human-powered central heating?"

She shook her head and shifted her feet. "Central heating's ancient history, Sam."

"People-heating?" he countered, and then laughed. "No, that's weird, even for 2221."

She took a step forward, dropping one of his hands so they could walk side by side. "Weird or not, we don't need to think about it. Much closer, and your cells won't be Lucian mutated."

"You told Dad yourself, it isn't guaranteed." He paused mid-stride. "Wait, if my cells return to normal, won't we both freeze?"

"That contingency has been planned for," the Commander broke in, his voice laced with static. "We have officers above the surface ready to break through and lift you out, if necessary."

"Too bad we couldn't beam up in a transporter," Sam remarked.

"Breaking up a person's molecules like that?" She laughed. "Definitely science fiction."

Static cracked in her communications circuit. "Commander still here. Update, Anderson?"

"I'm mobile now, Commander," Loretta said. "As we approach the center of the ice caverns, communications will likely fail. I'll keep an automatic log on my suit, but we won't be able to update you personally."

"I'll see what the officers on the surface can do to increase circuit strength," the Commander replied. "Continue high-frequency updates."

"Dad?" Sam said. "Are you and K'tor stable?"

"I'd estimate just above threshold," the Commander admitted. "Don't let that stop—"

As they slid across another patch of ice, the Commander's voice dropped out of the circuit. She almost lost her grip on Sam, but he swung her in a wide arc, and she hit the solid bank on the other side. Pulling him towards her, she looked over her shoulder.

"There's another cavern up ahead," she said, squinting hard even behind her visor. "The biggest and brightest yet." She paused and punched a button. The background whirr of assembling data filled her helmet, culminating in a rapid series of beeps.

"Are you sure your eyes aren't under strain?" Sam asked. "Looks like a black hole to me." His voice cracked, and she stared at him.

"The data automatically correlated, Sam. It's a cavern, dimensions—"

"I don't need dimensions," he interrupted. "But if it isn't a black hole—"

He didn't finish his sentence, and she reached for the scanner. "Off with the gloves, cadet. A cellular sample is in order once we reach the cavern."

He shuddered and turned away. "Loretta, I don't want to go in there."

She grabbed his shoulder and forced him to face her. "That's the doctor talking. Remember what Uncle Rob said? Don't let emotions run this expedition. What about the Vulcan?"

His smile twisted. "He's not saying much—my head's full of the doctor. Even the captain's not sure what to do."

She pulled off his gloves and initiated a contact sequence for one of his fingers. When the bio scanner collected a tissue sample, he didn't flinch.

"Okay, I'll handle the logic," she said. "K'tor inadvertently exposed you to a Lucian element that triggered widespread cellular change, mutation into a Lucian?" When Sam nodded, she continued, "And we deduced that exposure to the opposing element could counteract this mutation, correct?"

He nodded again as the scanner signaled completion. She read the data stream and slipped the scanner into her pocket.

"You can't live in temperature-controlled environments forever, Sam," she said softly. "We have to find a way to keep you stable, and this is the most probable solution."

He glanced at the entrance to the cavern. "But my Lucian cells—I can see their light now. And that cavern is so dark. And K'tor says—"

"Sam, you aren't a Lucian. You might feel like one, but you can't sustain the light they emanate."

"Who says I can't?" he retorted. "Biologically speaking, it's only logical—"

"Biologically speaking, you'll burn up if your environment doesn't counteract the phenomenon." She drew a deep breath. "Come on, I'll help you. One step at a time, okay?"

His shoulders slumped, but he reached for her hand. "The Vulcan admits that the cliché is logical. Successive steps are the only way to travel—at least in this case."

Facing him away from the cavern, she motioned for him to take a step back. "Count them, Sam. Don't let the people in your head have any say."

"One," Sam said, the word wavering a little. "Two. Three. Four."

She looked past him, over his shoulder, measuring the distance to the cavern. Before she could encourage him to keep counting, he broke the string of numbers.

"Loretta, I'm cold." He stumbled, but she steadied him. "Hot and cold at the same time."

Retrieving the scanner, she ran a non-contact sequence. "Your cellular structure hasn't changed, and your temperature is the same."

He frowned, then straightened his shoulders and took four more steps back. "How about now?"

"The same," she said. "Try stepping back until you feel normal—approximately normal."

"One. Two. Three. Four." Sam paused and shook his head. "One. Two. Three. How about here?"

She glanced down at the scanner, and then at Sam's feet. "Temperature still normal. Cells, no change. You're very close to—"

He didn't look down. "I think one more step should level out the temperature, at least psychologically. Ready?"

They moved together, her step forward and Sam's step back, so they stood hand-in-hand just inside the cavern. Sam swayed slightly, but she caught him before he fell.

"So cold, so cold," he whispered. "Why is it so cold?"

She felt her own fingers growing numb, but she fumbled for the scanner and initiated a contact sequence. The scanner settled on Sam's palm, which had stopped glowing.

"I won't let it have me," Sam shouted. "The darkness can't have me!"

The contact sequence ended. She lifted the scanner from Sam's palm, but her other hand still held his. The faint aura of light around his fingers reappeared, a soft glow against the piercing glint of the ice around them.

"You can't have me," Sam said, looking over his shoulder to stare down the cavern. "You can't have me, or Loretta—or anyone. You hear?"

The cavern echoed, and slivers of ice splintered off the walls, but Sam laughed.

"That's right," he said. "This may be a place of darkness, but not for me."

Sam's aura flashed—not a blinding glare of white light, but warm sunset light. She felt the heat flood through his hands into her numbed fingers. He laughed again and pulled her out of the cavern.

"The scanner?" he asked. His light faded slightly, but she could still see his grin.

She scrolled through the data and shook her head. "The cavern didn't alter your cells, at least not substantially."

His grin didn't waver. "But my temperature's steady, isn't it?"

She re-read the data and nodded. "Your cells are still producing light, but they aren't overheating. I can't isolate the element, but the cavern must have altered them."

Sam glanced back at the cavern. "I can see the outline of the cavern now, but it still looks like a black hole." He turned back to her with a somber smile. "Enough to counteract the light without destroying it."

"A stabilizing agent," she added, dropping his hand and sliding across an ice patch. "Hey, I don't need your hand to keep my fingers warm."

He took a running leap and slid ahead of her. "I don't think it's permanent. The flash will hold it, but you'll need your gloves soon."

"No people-heating?" she teased, jumping from one patch of ice to the next.

He raced ahead, doubling back in a narrow curve. "I don't think so. Multipurpose suits, complete with insulation, are here to stay. But—" At the edge of the ice patch, he stopped.

"Hey, what's with the human wall?" she asked, her visor knocking against his back.

"I can see Dad and K'tor up ahead," he said. "K'tor's light—it's going out."

Inside her helmet, the communication link clicked. "Loretta, Sam," the Commander said. "The Lucian is no longer stable, and I—"

"We're coming, Dad," Sam interrupted. "You're in sight, and K'tor too."

"The officers weren't able to come down, Sam. The ice was too thick, and we—"

"Dad, don't worry. I'm stable now, and I still have those Lucian perks. I'll get you mobile in no time, K'tor too."

"We're gliding toward you like those old-fashioned skaters, Uncle Rob," she added. "Count until we get there, okay? Don't think, just count."

"One. Two." The Commander's voice steadied. "Three. Four."

They almost flew across the last stretch of ice. "Keep counting, Dad," Sam said, sliding to a stop beside the Commander. "Loretta's going to take your gloves, and I'll—just wait."

She unfastened the Commander's gloves, and Sam took his father's hands. His aura flashed and for a moment the sun seemed to set in the ice below the earth.

"How's this for stable, Dad?" Sam asked. "Not so cold?"

The Commander shook his head. "Not cold at all," he said. "I'm surprised the ice isn't melting."

K'tor's light brightened, almost blinding her, but Sam didn't flinch. She couldn't follow the flood of Lucian words, and Sam held up a still-glowing hand.

"I have your light, but I do not have your words," he said, shifting languages. "Is the light strong in you now?"

K'tor's light flashed again. "Yes, the light is strong. But I do not understand, Sam. You went to the staying-place of the darkness, and still you have the light?"

Sam shook his head. "I do not understand, K'tor. Only that the darkness did not take me, and I have the light." He looked from K'tor to Loretta, shifting back to his usual speech. "If I'm the world's first human-Lucian hybrid—"

"A space cadet alien hybrid? That's definitely a new entry for my panzoölogy index." she said. "Sounds a bit like a superhero to me."

He grinned. "Every superhero needs a sidekick. Are you volunteering?" When she made a face at him, he added. "I would really be like the Vulcan, half-Lucian and half-human."

"Half-Lucian or not, you're still a cadet," the Commander intervened. "Hybrid status doesn't guarantee a promotion—but saving a commander's life just might."

Sam shook his head. "Only if you say so, sir. I can do plenty, even as a cadet."

Loretta couldn't help smiling as she translated the conversation for K'tor.

"Yes, Sam will do much," he said, his light flaring. "The Lucians who have little light, from the staying-place of the dark, he will bring them his light. And he will do even more than this—you will see."

The Commander smiled. "I'm sure you will, Robinson—and do it carefully."

Sam grinned. "Of course, sir. If I wasn't careful, where would I be today?"

"I can think of several safer places," she interjected. "Earth, for example."

"Earth?" he echoed. "Where's the adventure there? I'd rather be a Lucian on GT-937."

"Well, isn't that lucky?" She pulled him into a hug, light aura and all. "Because that's exactly where you are."

### *Sky for Sam*

"Mrs. Anderson? There's a message for you, visual included. I can play it inside if you—"

She rocked back in her chair, the antique with the wooden runners, and tilted her head. The porch creaked when she moved, the porch she'd made them keep.

"Never mind about the message, Alice. Why don't you watch the stars with me?"

Alice laughed, the polite laugh they were both used to. "Mrs. Anderson, you watch the stars every night. This is a message from Sam."

She looked away from the pinpricks of light. "A message from Sam? Doesn't he write me?"

Alice nodded. "Yes, ma'am, but he's given you something to look at this time."

She stood up, creaking almost as much as the porch. "I suppose that means you can't get that fancy machine to give me a piece of paper with his writing on it, can you?"

Alice smiled and turned to open the screen door. "No, ma'am, I can't. The computer can retranslate code into handwriting, but visuals are visuals."

She held up her hands. The porch light outlined every crease crisscrossing her skin. "Well, I grant the machine that. Let's go see what Sam looks like now, shall we?"

Alice held open the screen door for her, and she walked into the kitchen, trying not to shuffle across the battered linoleum. A light flickered on when they entered, but she ignored the automated readout that announced the inner climate controls. At the door to the living room, she stopped with her hand on the warped doorjamb.

"Alice, can't we keep that off? If I'm expected to live with these newfangled gadgets—"

Alice laid a hand on her shoulder, guiding her into the room and across the worn carpet. The automatic lights blinked on, but Alice switched them off and circled the room to turn on the lamps instead.

"Mrs. Anderson, these 'gadgets' are over two hundred years old. Even you—"

"Aren't that old," she finished, with a wry smile. "I know, Alice, I know." She settled into her understuffed armchair and reached for her usual afghan, lacing her fingers through the knitted holes.

"Are you sure you don't want to give that to a museum, or maybe one of our research teams?" Alice asked. "That's really where it belongs."

She blew out her breath, sharply. "It belongs with me. You know I don't like these synthetics, Alice. When I die—"

Alice smiled. "Don't worry, I'll keep it for you. I'm only asking because I have to."

She tucked the afghan across her lap. "I know, my dear, I know."

As the visual transmitter powered up, she tried to ignore the insistent hum of machinery. Alice's fingers skated across the control board, pressing here and there until the screen turned from dead black to uncertain gray.

"Alice—" She shifted in her chair.

Alice pressed another button, and a timestamp formed on the screen. "Do you need something? We can watch this another time, if you're tired."

She shook her head. "No, I'd like to see Sam. But Alice—" She searched for the right words. "I'm sorry that you have to do this. I've gone on long enough not to be sorry for myself, but for you to be here—"

Alice turned away from the transmitter, towards her, and smiled. "Oh, I don't mind. Would I have requested this assignment if I didn't want it?"

She smiled in return. "I suppose not. But a bright girl like you, you should be out there." Glancing up at the peaked ceiling, she added, "Up there, like Sam and Loretta, exploring. An astronaut."

Alice laughed, the one she used when she really meant to laugh. "They don't call them that anymore, but I never wanted to be one. I like the old things, you know."

She chuckled, a creaky laugh. "So caring for this living piece of history is just your cup of tea, isn't it?" Reaching for the lamp beside her chair, she pulled the beaded chain to extinguish the light.

Alice pressed the transmitter's last button, and Sam's face replaced the timestamp.

"Hello to the word's best Grandmam from GT-937!" His voice scratched and creaked almost as much as hers, but she smiled. "Cadet Sam Robinson reporting."

She leaned forward in her chair. "Reporting, are you? Well, go on."

Sam grinned. "I'm sorry we can't do this in real time, but the communications delay would be ages. We're pretty far out—you know that already." He glanced down at his hands, and she stared a little harder at the screen.

"You're probably wondering why I didn't just write you," he continued. "I thought about it, but I also thought you might want to see this. Remember the Lucians I told you about?"

She nodded, forgetting that he couldn't answer. "Those aliens, the ones that have their own shine."

"They're called 'life forms,'" Alice corrected gently, "and they emit light, Mrs. Anderson."

Sam laughed. "Alice is probably correcting your terminology, so I gave her a second." He glanced down at his hands again, and then back up. "I had an adventure with these Lucians. The details aren't important, but it changed me."

She clutched her afghan a little tighter. "Sam—"

"I'm fine, I'm really fine," he assured her. "Loretta can send you all my scans, if you want. There was a time when I—wasn't, but I'm fine now."

He held up his hands, and she blinked, hard. "Sam, are your hands—"

"Glowing," he finished. "Yeah, they are. I'm still as human as you are, but I've turned half-Lucian too. I have a shine like they do, and I can see them easier." He dropped his hands and smiled. "Dad calls it a great scientific breakthrough."

"Well, does he?" She sat back in her chair. "Jacob calls plenty of things scientific. He was always the grandson messing with—"

"You're probably grumbling about Dad," Sam interrupted. "That's okay, he doesn't mind. We all think you're wonderful. But Grandmam—"

"Yes?" She sat forward in her chair, and the afghan slid to the floor.

"The Lucian part of me makes it hard to see the stars." He smiled again, but without his grin. "There's so much light, and their sky can get cloudy as fast as an April thunderstorm. So I was wondering—could you send me some of the stars from your place?"

She laced her fingers together. "Sam, I don't—"

"It isn't that hard, Grandmam." He clasped his glowing hands behind his back. "Just head out to that porch of yours. Alice will help you send the transmission, and all you have to do is say, 'Hello, Sam. Here are the stars.'"

She stood slowly, still watching his face.

"And Grandmam?" He leaned forward. "It would be nice to see you." Then he dropped his hands to his sides. "Cadet Robinson, reporting out from GT-937. Lots of love, from Sam."

The transmitter screen faded to gray. She drew a deep breath as Alice reached for the lamp. The light clicked on, and they blinked in the warm glow.

"Well, Alice?" she said. "I suppose you are going to watch the stars with me, after all."

## *Appendices*
## GT-937 Timeline

2100 c—Marcus and Sarai Dallen meet aboard the lunar colony

2150 May 25—Peter Dallen dies collecting data on *Titan*'s asteroid mission

2151 December 14—Loretta comes out of suspension, aged 21

2220 January—Loretta comes to GT-937 on *Lightfoot*, builds relationships with Lucians

2220 November 28-December 31—Sam writes to his Grandmam (Loretta, aged 91)

## Reedsy Prompts

"Sunset Moon" Contest 52: Every year, one person is sent to the moon. This year, though you hid in terror, it is your turn to enter the rocket.

"Blood Moon" Contest 75: Write about two characters who each want to change the same thing, but resolve to go about it in very different ways.

"Mission 404" Contest 76: Write a story told exclusively through dialogue.

"Resolution" Contest 76: Write a conversation that takes place between two people who refuse to say what they mean.

"Connection" Contest 76: Write about a character who's always thinking of things they'll say to people, but who ends up saying very little when they finally get the chance.

"Suspension" Contest 76: Write about a character who is incapable of telling even the smallest lie or half-truth.

"Earth Setting" Contest 39: Write about a person experiencing the 'overview effect' (a feeling astronauts report having when they first view Earth from outer space).

"Sun Setting" Contest 39: One day, the sun rose in the west and set in the east.

"Essential Threesome" Contest 42: Write a story that ends with a character asking a question.

"Traveling to Infinity" originally published as "Light Chameleon" Contests 44: Write a story that starts with a character-revealing something unusual about themselves. 45: Write a story about change. 46: Write a story about someone experiencing a lightbulb moment of writing inspiration. 48: Write about someone who has a superpower.

"Sky for Sam" Contest 51: Write a story that begins and ends with someone looking up at the stars.

Ingram Content Group UK Ltd.
Milton Keynes UK
UKHW020635060623
422954UK00014B/705